"All you

Evan whispered to himself as he got off the elevator.

Admitting how dependent his family was on Claire and recognizing how close he'd come to alienating her earlier, he knew he had to be on his best behavior. He couldn't yell at her or accuse her of things. And he certainly couldn't be attracted to her....

He pushed open the door, and she turned and smiled. "Hi."

Evan's breath froze in his lungs. Her clinging powder-blue knit dress outlined every delicious curve of her body, accented her brilliant sapphire-blue eyes and brought each of Evan's nerve endings to complete attention.

He tried reminding himself of all the good reasons he had to stomp out this attraction, but in the end, he knew it was a losing battle....

* * *

**Don't miss this 1st book in
THE BREWSTER BABY BOOM trilogy!
Next month is *Bringing Up Babies* (SR #1427)
And in late March is *Oh Babies!* (SR #1433)**

Dear Reader,

The year 2000 marks the twentieth anniversary of Silhouette Books! Ever since May 1980, Silhouette Books—and its flagship line, Silhouette Romance—has published the best in contemporary category romance fiction. And the year's stellar lineups across *all* Silhouette series continue that tradition.

This month in Silhouette Romance, Susan Meier unveils her miniseries BREWSTER BABY BOOM, in which three brothers confront instant fatherhood after inheriting six-month-old triplets! First up is *The Baby Bequest*, in which Evan Brewster does diaper duty…and learns a thing or two about love from his much-younger, mommy-in-the-making assistant. In Teresa Southwick's charming new Silhouette Romance novel, a tall, dark and handsome man decides to woo a jaded nurse *With a Little T.L.C. The Sheik's Solution* is a green-card marriage to his efficient secretary in this lavish fairy tale from Barbara McMahon.

Elizabeth Harbison's CINDERELLA BRIDES series continues with the magnificent *Annie and the Prince*. In Cara Colter's dramatic *A Babe in the Woods*, a mystery man arrives on a reclusive woman's doorstep with a babe on his back—and a gun in his backpack! Then we have a man without a memory who returns to his *Prim, Proper… Pregnant* former fiancée—this unique story by Alice Sharpe is a must-read for those who love twists and turns.

In coming months, look for special titles by longtime favorites Diana Palmer, Joan Hohl, Kasey Michaels, Dixie Browning, Phyllis Halldorson and Tracy Sinclair, as well as many newer but equally loved authors. It's an exciting year for Silhouette Books, and we invite you to join the celebration!

Happy reading!

Mary-Theresa Hussey

Mary-Theresa Hussey
Senior Editor

Please address questions and book requests to:
Silhouette Reader Service
U.S.: 3010 Walden Ave., P.O. Box 1325, Buffalo, NY 14269
Canadian: P.O. Box 609, Fort Erie, Ont. L2A 5X3

THE BABY BEQUEST

Susan Meier

Silhouette

R O M A N C E™

Published by Silhouette Books

America's Publisher of Contemporary Romance

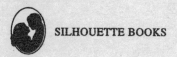

SILHOUETTE BOOKS

ISBN 0-373-19420-X

THE BABY BEQUEST

This edition published by arrangement with Harlequin Books S.A.

® and TM are trademarks of Harlequin Books S.A., used under license.
Trademarks indicated with ® are registered in the United States Patent
and Trademark Office, the Canadian Trade Marks Office and in other
countries.

Visit us at www.romance.net

Printed in U.S.A.

Books by Susan Meier

Silhouette Romance

Stand-in Mom #1022
Temporarily Hers #1109
Wife in Training #1184
Merry Christmas, Daddy #1192
In Care of the Sheriff #1283
Guess What? We're Married! #1338
Husband from 9 to 5 #1354
The Rancher and the Heiress #1374
†*The Baby Bequest* #1420

*Texas Family Ties
†Brewster Baby Boom

Silhouette Desire

Take the Risk #567

SUSAN MEIER

has written ten category romances for Silhouette
Romance and Silhouette Desire. A full-time writer,
Susan has been an employee of a major defense contrac-
tor, a columnist for a small newspaper and a division
manager of a charitable organization. But her greatest
joy in her life has always been her children, who constantly surprise and amaze her. Married for twenty years
to her wonderful, understanding and gorgeous husband,
Michael, Susan cherishes her roles as a mother, wife, sister and friend, believing them to be life's real treasures.
She not only cherishes those roles as gifts, she tries to
convey the beauty and importance of loving relationships
in her books.

Dear Evan,

There isn't a day that goes by that I don't think of you and your brothers and the unfortunate split in our family.

Nonetheless, if anything ever happens to me, no matter what your feelings, you and your brothers must become guardians to your half siblings. I have faith that the three of you will do the right thing.

You, however, must also take full responsibility for the lumber mill. Though Grant may be the most stable, and Chas may be the most crafty, because you have special sensibilities, you are my choice to sit at the helm of my business. I know I don't need to remind you that a man's worth isn't necessarily in the obvious. We may have made this community by providing jobs and a source of pride for the people of this county, but the truth is, this community made us. We owe them. They are stakeholders in our business every bit as much as we are. I want you to take care of them.

And I also want you to do right by my assistant, Claire. If you keep her on as your helpmate, she'll not only teach you the ropes of the business and do a good day's work for you every day, but she might just teach you a thing or two about yourself.

Love always,

Dad

Chapter One

Claire Wilson opened the door of Attorney Arnie Garrett's office and a little bell rang, announcing her arrival.

"Good afternoon, Claire," Jennifer Raymond, Arnie's secretary, called from around a corner. "I know that's you," she said, "because everyone else is already gathered in the conference room. Mr. Garrett's not back from the funeral yet. So you can either wait in the reception area or go down the hall and join the other interested parties."

Claire licked her dry lips. She knew who the other "interested parties" for the reading of Norm Brewster's will were. Norm's sons—Evan, Chas and Grant. In this little corner of the world they weren't merely part of the family that founded Brewster County, Pennsylvania, they were notorious. After years of spending the family fortune like water, wreaking havoc on the virtue of the local girls and using their fists to prove most of their points, all three had walked away from Brewster County two years ago, vowing never to return.... Rumor had it they'd gone on a two-year binge of sin and corruption.

"You wouldn't be standing there making rash judgments, now, would you?"

Claire jumped at the sound of Jennifer's voice and spun around.

"I'm not making any sort of judgments at all," Claire lied.

"Oh, baloney," Arnie's secretary said with a wave of her slender hand. She was a tall woman, at least five-ten. Her gray hair was pulled into a loose knot at her nape and her blue eyes sparkled with the joy of the moment. "Everybody's making judgments and speculations," she whispered as she cautiously approached Claire. "It's been a mystery to everyone why Norm chose to marry a woman half his age only two months after his first wife's death. When they ran, those boys weren't doing anything but being loyal to their mother."

Having seen how Norm Brewster had pined for his sons Claire had her own opinion about that, but she didn't care to share it with Brewster County's official gossip hotline. She edged her way around Jennifer to the doorway. "Uh, you said everybody was in the conference room, right? I think I will join them."

Walking down the dimly lit corridor, she heard the low rumblings of male voices only a few feet away from her and her stomach did a somersault. Because these men were much older than she was, she knew about them by reputation only, but the rumors she'd heard were enough to scare anyone witless. And, too, these men had hurt Norm, a man she'd grown to care for and admire.

Still, she drew in a deep breath and headed for her first meeting with the Brewster brothers. She was going to have to face them sooner or later, because if what she suspected was true, the reading of the will would announce that these three were her new bosses.

"Gentlemen," she said as she breezed in and walked to a chair at the end of the table.

Instantly, all three men stopped talking.

"I'm Claire Wilson," she continued, struggling to keep her voice from shaking. Her heart constricted painfully, then began to pound in her chest. The Brewster boys were big, much bigger than she'd expected. And handsome. Dressed in dark suits, white shirts and ties, they looked respectable and sophisticated, but there was still something rough and dangerous about them. Any female over the age of fifteen could easily understand why women dropped at the feet of these men.

One had eyes so dark they were nearly black, and dark hair. The other two were almost his opposite with sandy brown hair and pale-colored eyes. Both of them gave her a suspicious, somewhat hostile scrutiny because she'd invaded their privacy.

Claire's breath shivered in her chest. "I am...was...your father's assistant at Brewster Lumber," she explained.

Finally, after what seemed a century of silence, one of the lighter-haired men spoke. "It's nice to meet you, Miss Wilson."

"Thank you," she said softly, then swallowed hard. She couldn't tell if she was afraid of these men or attracted to them, or both. All she really knew was they had presence. Rumors and stories she'd heard as a teenager took on new meaning.

"I'm Evan," he said, walking toward her with his hand extended.

Claire swallowed again. "I'm sorry about your loss," she said as she allowed him to wrap her small hand in his much larger one. Up close he was even bigger than he seemed from across the room. And much more imposing. Not only could she smell the fresh, spicy scent of his aftershave, but she could see that his eyes were green. Cool, misty green.

Before Evan Brewster had a chance to reply, Arnie Garrett bounded into the room. "I see you're meeting everyone, Claire," he said as he strode to the head of the table, his arms piled high with file folders stuffed to capacity. His short gray hair was tousled in spite of the fact that there was no breeze on this bright May day, and his suit was oddly wrinkled.

"You're shaking Evan's hand," Arnie continued. "The dark-haired gentleman is Grant. And the last, here, is Chas." He paused and smiled at the three men, all of whom suddenly looked sheepish and docile. "Everybody take a seat anywhere around the table," he directed as he began rummaging through the top file. "Claire, you remember witnessing Mr. Brewster's will last summer?"

"Yes," she said, though she didn't believe her witnessing Norm's signature was the reason she'd been summoned. Norm had asked for the favor on her second day of employment, and she hadn't seen the specifics of the document.

"Well, there's been a codicil," Arnie said as he carried the instrument to Claire and motioned for her to identify her signature.

She nodded.

"The codicil doesn't change anything, only adds to

it," he explained as he returned to his chair. "When the will is officially probated, you, Jennifer and I will need to go to the Register of Wills office and sign papers. For now, though, this is nothing more than an informal reading."

Claire relaxed, but as she did she glanced over and saw Evan studying her, his elbow resting on the arm of his chair and his cheek braced between his index finger and thumb. He was a beautiful man, a perfect specimen. His thick sandy-brown hair fell in a soft wave to his forehead and had enough body that it stayed where he combed it. His skin had a very natural, healthy tone that emphasized his opaque eyes. His nose was the right size and shape for his face, and his lips were full, his mouth generous. She'd never, ever seen anybody who was as flawless as he was—at least not in person.

"So, we'll get right to the will, because it's relatively short and uncomplicated. Then I'll move into the additions of the codicil."

Arnie's sudden announcement caused Claire to realize she was staring at Evan Brewster, and she quickly looked away. She thought that he should have been embarrassed for staring at her, as well, but in a swift peek she saw he obviously wasn't. He was curious about her and he didn't feel the need to hide it.

Well, let him be curious. Lord knew, everybody was curious enough about him. If her guess was correct, the Brewster boys now owned Brewster Lumber. Even if they decided to sell it, they'd have to spend a few weeks around town, and Claire knew Evan Brewster would get more than his fair share of stares.

"Claire?"

Claire started as if in a trance. "I'm sorry," she apologized to Arnie. "I didn't hear what you said."

"I said that the first item in the codicil is a bequest from Mr. Brewster to you of ten thousand dollars."

Claire pressed her hand to her throat. "Oh."

"You are the only beneficiary outside of the family," Arnie noted, smiling fondly at her.

"Which explains her presence here," Evan said, sounding irritated.

"Evan," Arnie cautioned. "I also invited Claire to be here this morning so that I could introduce her to all of you because she was your father's assistant. If the three of you are going to take over Brewster Lumber, she's the person you need most in the world right now. You know your father didn't employ any executives. He didn't have a board of directors. He did everything himself, hoping for the day one or all of you would return home. Because he wanted to be able to give each of you a position at the mill, he couldn't give those jobs to other people. So, with Claire's help, he ran the business himself."

Claire watched quietly as all three brothers exhibited a range of complex emotions. Grant hung his head guiltily. Chas drew in a long breath. Evan gazed out the window. If the expression on his face was any gauge, it appeared he wished he could live the last two years over again.

If she didn't know how much Norm had suffered from his sons' rejection, Claire might have actually felt sorry for them. But she did know how lonely and abandoned he'd felt. And these men were the cause of that pain.

"Because I'm familiar with all the circumstances of this situation, I recognize this isn't easy for you,"

Arnie continued delicately. "But I also know that your father would want nothing more than to see the three of you at home again, taking your place at Brewster Lumber. I'm proud of all of you for coming home."

Evan cleared his throat. "It's a little late."

Arnie shook his head. "Not really. All your father ever wanted was for Brewster Lumber to continue on. You could still fulfill his wishes."

Though Claire understood that coddling these three was probably Arnie's way of cajoling them into staying in town, she still agreed with Evan. It *was* a little late—about two years too late. As far as she was concerned, the fact that they'd been "kind" enough to come home to take possession of the highly successful family business didn't do much in the way of exonerating them.

Arnie set the will on the table. "The rest of the codicil revolves around one specific thing. Before I move on, I'd like to know if you have any questions about what I've already read."

"I don't think there is anything to explain. Even if I wasn't a lawyer, I'd know that because our stepmother died in the accident with our father, we inherit the lumber mill," Chas said softly.

"That's right," Arnie agreed. "Actually, the codicil stipulates that you inherit all your family's holdings, including the house, equally with your siblings."

"Brothers," Chas corrected absently, nervously tapping a pencil he'd pulled from his jacket pocket. Though he had similar coloring to Evan, the two really didn't look alike. Chas had a more boyish face. Evan, with his cool, direct stare and very angular cheekbones, looked older, wiser...sexier.

"No, Chas," Arnie said haltingly. "I didn't make a mistake. And neither did your father when this addition was written. He said siblings because he meant siblings."

"But we only have brothers," Evan quietly observed, piercing Arnie with his uncompromising gaze.

"Actually, you don't," Arnie said. He rose from his seat, pressed a button on the telephone and instructed Jennifer to come into the office.

Claire got a sick feeling in her stomach. It had never occurred to her that because Norm's sons hadn't spoken to him in two years, they didn't know their father had *triplets!*

Grinning from ear to ear, Jennifer entered carrying two adorable little girls, one on the crook of each arm. Both were around six months old and were dressed in pink ruffled dresses with white tights and black Mary Janes.

"My God, twins!" Grant gasped.

"No. Triplets!" Jennifer all but sang, stepping out of the way and allowing everyone to see Arnie's wife, Judy, as she walked into the room carrying a little boy. Wearing a miniature suit and tie, he was every bit as beautiful as his two sisters. But not only were the three children darling, they were also picture-perfect matches for the Brewster brothers. One of the girls had black hair and dark eyes. The second girl and the boy had light brown hair and pale green eyes.

For the next thirty seconds, Evan felt as if all the air had been drained from the room as he struggled to comprehend that he had not only another brother— a *baby* brother—but two sisters, as well.

Sisters!

He pressed his hands to his face, then rubbed them down his cheeks. What had his father done?

"Angela wasn't pregnant when Dad married her, was she?" Grant asked angrily.

Because that was an excellent question, Evan came to attention.

"No, the kids are only six months old."

"And they're that big?" Chas gasped.

"They're actually average size," Jennifer happily said as she brought the girls farther into the room. Walking around the table, she eased the dark-haired baby onto Grant's lap and then handed the other girl to Evan. Judy gave the boy to Chas.

Awestruck, confused, numb, Evan stared at the little girl, who took one look at him and let out a screaming wail. Purely on instinct, he grabbed her under the arms and held her away from him. "I swear to God, I didn't hurt her."

"She's only frightened," Judy soothed as she set the baby girl on Evan's lap again. "She needs to get to know you. Give her a few minutes to get familiar with you and she won't cry anymore."

As the words came out of Judy's mouth, the real meaning of what she was saying hit Evan, and he glanced at Chas, whose wide-eyed stare told him he'd also figured everything out, then at Grant, who also had a glazed expression in his brown eyes.

Evan looked down at his little sister. A child. A baby. *Babies.* "These kids are our responsibility now, aren't they?"

Arnie nodded once. "I'm afraid so."

"My God, he peed on me!" Chas cried, and bounced from his seat, holding the baby away from him as if that could protect his already damp trousers.

At his sudden movement, though, all three babies started to cry and scream.

"Unfortunately, I'm not very good with these disposable diapers yet," Judy confessed, shouting to be heard over the noise. "My babies wore cloth diapers and plastic pants. I'm afraid this was the best I could do."

"Since the accident, my wife and I have been caring for the children," Arnie explained. "But I researched the law and the bottom line is that the triplets belong to you."

Though Grant and Chas looked completely confused and out of their element, Evan felt wave upon wave of an emotion he couldn't begin to identify. All his life he'd wanted children. Doctor after doctor told him he couldn't have children. Now, when he'd all but given up hope, his father had given him the one thing he couldn't give himself. A family. Babies. And not just one or two...three. Three glorious children.

His throat closed and he swallowed convulsively. "What do you mean you researched the law?" he asked quietly, finally realizing what Arnie had said didn't fit in with the rest of the conversation.

"Let's face it, Evan," Arnie said. "You're three single men. I don't think you're the best choice for guardians. I wanted to be sure that legally you were the people who were *supposed* to be the guardians, so I did some checking. And the law says these children are yours, unless you want to—"

"Unless we want to what?" Chas said with cool tones.

"Sign over custody," Arnie said casually. "I have papers right here. All you have to do is sign them and Judy and I will continue to take care of the kids."

Evan knew he should have let Chas handle this, since he was a lawyer, but something inside him snapped. *These were* his *kids, damn it! They were Brewsters and they would be raised by Brewsters.*

Even as his baby sister screamed and squirmed in his arms—or maybe *because* she screamed and squirmed in his arms—Evan got the distinct impression he and his brothers had been set up by his father's best friend and attorney. He didn't think it was a coincidence that Arnie asked them to sign over custody two minutes after he told them of the children's existence and while all three babies screamed bloody murder.

"Why would you think we would want to hand over custody?" he asked, hanging on to his temper only by the merest of threads.

"Well, look at you," Arnie scoffed, but kindly. "The three of you aren't prepared to be parents, least of all to triplets."

"Is that why no one bothered to mention the children when we arrived this morning?" Chas asked angrily.

"Well, I... The shock of your father's death was enough," Arnie said logically. "I couldn't spring it on you that you also had two sisters and a brother."

"Who also inherit half the lumber mill," Grant surmised, rising. "I guess that never crossed your mind when you decided you wanted custody."

Evan was glad his brothers could think so clearly, so rationally, but it was also apparent that their tempers were reaching the point where there would be no turning back. With three screaming babies and two furious, conclusion-jumping brothers on his hands, Evan knew it was time to leave before somebody said something he might regret. His own notions about Arnie's motives were making him every bit as angry as his brothers appeared to be. But more than that, the subtle insinuation that *maybe* their father wouldn't want them to have the kids was pushing him over the edge. He couldn't believe that. He *refused* to believe that. Because his father was the only person aside from doctors who knew Evan couldn't have children, Evan wouldn't believe his father would be so cruel as to deny him the privilege of raising these three.

In fact, that was his saving grace. That was the minute when he forgave his father, and in his heart knew he'd try to understand. Because his father had stipulated in his will that the brothers were to be guardians, Evan knew he had not only forgiven his sons, he was allowing the family to move on.

Lord only knew what Arnie Garrett was trying to pull.

Evan rose. "Are there diapers or bottles or something that we should have?"

"I have a diaper bag in the office," Judy said uncertainly.

"Good, please get it. Chas, Grant, let's go."

"Now, wait," Arnie said, trying to stop them.

Already at the door, Evan spun around. "No, you wait," he angrily countered. "I don't give a damn what you think about me or my brothers, but you had no right to second-guess my father's wishes for these children. Whether you like it or not, Mr. Garrett, Brewsters take care of their own. And if my father were alive, that's exactly what he'd tell you. He'd stand by his will."

Judy returned and handed the huge diaper bag to

Evan. He easily hoisted the strap of the satchel over one shoulder.

"Evan, wait," Arnie called, but Evan kept walking. He managed to snuggle his baby sister closer to his chest, and though that didn't entirely calm her, at least it took her crying to a low wail. He strode down the hall, then through the front office and the door with the tinkling bell and out into the sunshine, his brothers behind him.

"Evan, wait!"

This time the call came from Claire, the assistant. And that was another thing. Ten thousand dollars to a woman who was an assistant for a year? One short year? Evan didn't begrudge his father the right to do what he wanted to do with his money, but given that Arnie had tried to sneak the kids away from him everything in that codicil became suspicious.

"Wait!"

This call was louder and stronger and gave Evan the impression she planned on following him forever if she needed to. Rather than take her to the door of the Brewster mansion, he stopped.

"What?" he demanded angrily.

She drew a long breath because she'd been running, and Evan tried not to notice the flush on her cheeks or the way her silky black hair accented her blue eyes.

"Car seats," she managed to say when she'd finally gotten enough air.

He stared at her. "Car seats?"

"In Pennsylvania it's the law that all kids under the age of four have to be in a car seat."

Evan looked at Chas.

"She's right," Chas said, juggling the little boy he held in an effort to get him to stop crying.

Evan hesitated a few seconds. "I'm only going three miles up the road," he said, and turned away from Claire. "I will drive safely and I will drive slowly. Once we get the kids settled, I'll send Grant out for car seats."

He felt a tug on his coat sleeve and, annoyed, stopped again. "What?"

"This is ridiculous," she said softly, infuriatingly calm. "All we have to do is take these kids back to Arnie's office and get their car seats from Judy's car."

Evan didn't care that what she said made sense. What he felt was fresh and raw. He knew the bottom line for Arnie was probably money, and the thought that someone would use children for profit made Evan sick. Going back for those car seats was a capitulation he knew he couldn't make. Particularly since he didn't have any idea what Claire's involvement was in this situation. She might be innocently drawing him back for car seats, or she might be taking them back to give Arnie another shot at getting the guardianship release signed.

He gave her a cool look. "We'll stop at the discount store on the outskirts of town. That means we'll be driving about a mile without car seats, but we'll get the car seats," he said quietly, protectively clutching his sister. He didn't even care when she wiped her wet nose on his lapel. "If you don't like that, call the police."

With that he turned away again and started down Market Street toward his sport utility vehicle, which was parked by the curb. Because both Grant and Chas had ridden with him, the three men and their babies stopped when they reached Evan's truck. He unlocked the doors.

helping Arnie out of loyalty to his father, which meant it had to be naïveté.

To a degree, Evan could accept that. Claire was young. And pretty enough that she'd probably been protected from the harsh realities of life by doting parents, idealistic teachers and every man in this county.

He scowled, confused about why that twisted oddly in his gut. The girl was a looker. There was no sense pretending she didn't have boys knocking down her door....

Furious with himself for thinking about foolish things when he had real trouble to attend to, Evan scowled again and shoved the woman out of his mind as he jogged up the steps of the circular stairway in the foyer of the Brewster mansion.

He and his brothers had accidentally discovered the nursery when they'd gone in search of the birth certificates, the will and its codicil. Eventually they found all three in their father's safe. Everything Arnie had told them that morning had been verified—including the fact that if the Brewster sons didn't want custody of the triplets, Arnie and Judy Garrett would be the guardians. As such, Arnie would be the trustee of their holdings in Brewster Lumber, and he would have fifty percent voting power and complete control of the triplets' money. He'd also be paid a handsome salary. Reason enough, in Evan's mind, for the man to try to get custody of the children.

When Evan opened the nursery door, a cacophony of crying greeted him like the noise of an off-key symphony. If he hadn't been so frazzled trying to figure things out—like the kids' names, how to get them to stop crying, and how to feed them—he would have taken a moment just to absorb everything. Their little faces, the reality that they were his flesh and blood kin, the fact that they were sisters and a brother were almost incomprehensible.

"Give me a damned bottle already," Grant growled as Evan made his way into the nursery. Fading rays of late-afternoon sunshine poured into the curtainless windows at the back of the room, which was already bright and cheerful with white walls covered with radiant rainbows. Carefully neutral, the nursery had obviously been designed to keep the kids together without insulting Norm Brewster's sensibilities about little boys being anywhere near pink.

Remembering his father, Evan held back an involuntary smile, which turned into a surge of pain and regret. How he wished he could have these last two years back again. If nothing else, he would at least *try* to understand why his father had married so soon after his wife's death…and why he married someone so young…and why he had more children.

"A bottle, Evan," Chas implored in exasperation, and Evan brought himself out of his reverie, knowing it was pointless to wish for things that couldn't happen.

Both Grant and Chas sat in rockers, each holding a fussing baby. The third child sat in the crib, clutching the bars, sobbing as she awaited Evan's return.

"Okay, one bottle for Taylor," he said, and handed it to Grant. "One for Annie," he said, using the shortened version of Antoinette. "And one bottle for Cody."

Taylor almost grabbed the bottle from Grant's hands and gulped the contents as if she had been on a deserted island without food for the past two days.

Little Annie also drank quickly and easily, nearly directing Evan on how to handle the bottle. But Chas had the devil's time getting Cody to drink. Chas would move one way, Cody would move the other. The nipple bumped his nose. Chas dripped liquid on Cody's forehead. And all the while the starving baby screamed.

"This isn't going to work," Chas growled after he'd finally made contact with Cody's mouth.

"Yes, it is," Evan insisted doggedly.

"You can't raise kids on good intentions," Chas said as he set his rocker in motion.

"We have more than good intentions," Evan said, beginning to rock after he was sure Annie was comfortable.

"We don't know the first thing about babies."

"Gentlemen," Grant interjected. "In case you didn't notice this morning, we had a volunteer to assist us. Unfortunately, somebody insisted we didn't need her."

"I don't think we do."

"Well, *I* think we do," Grant said simply.

"And *I* think we do," Chas agreed, then he bounced off his chair. "Aw, damn. He spit up on me." Turning his head slowly, Chas speared Evan with a withering look. "I *know* we need help."

"Then go ahead and call her," Evan said, refusing to use Claire's name because he got a fluttery sensation in the pit of his stomach when he realized he'd get to see her again. Which was insane. She was ten years younger than he was. And potentially up to her ears in Arnie Garrett's scheme to take the triplets.

He couldn't possibly be attracted to her.

It wasn't right.

"Uh-uh." Chas shook head. "You yelled at her, you call her."

"I agree with Chas," Grant said, rocking Taylor, who sucked noisily. "You yelled at her, you call her."

"You boys forget, I don't think we need her."

"And you forget, Evan, that Arnie Garrett has a lot to gain if he becomes guardian for these kids," Chas reminded his brother. "Having a will or even having the law on our side won't mean anything if Arnie can prove we're incompetent. I say we call her."

Evan looked down and saw that little Annie had finished her bottle and was peacefully sleeping in his arms. Taylor was nearly asleep in Grant's arms, and even Cody had settled down and was drinking heartily.

They didn't need help from anyone.

This baby thing was a piece of cake....

As she unlocked the door of her apartment that night, Claire could hear her phone ringing. She juggled two bags of groceries and quickly pushed her way into her kitchen, catching the phone on the fourth ring.

"Hello," she said breathlessly.

"Hello, this is Evan Brewster."

Claire felt an incomprehensible torrent of pleasure just hearing his voice. Which was ridiculous. He might be a handsome man, but he was a stubborn man, an angry man and one of her new bosses.

Still, her traitorous, disobedient heart skipped a beat. Claire ignored it in favor of more important concerns like why was Evan calling her? Was it to fire her for slamming a car door in his face earlier? Or was it to ask for help? She prayed he was calling for help.

"What's up?" she asked, trying to sound casual as she angled the phone between her ear and shoulder.

There was a pause. A long one. Finally, Evan said, "We could really use some guidance with the kids."

Claire released a silent sigh of relief. Thanks to the triplets, it appeared she was keeping her job. Norm had always said they were an unexpected blessing. She was beginning to understand what he meant. "Tell me what's wrong and I'll tell you how to fix it."

"We figured out how to use the disposable diapers, but the same system that works for the girls doesn't seem to work for Cody. All the things Judy gave us are gone. We don't know if we're allowed to feed them anything besides what was in the bottles, and we can't get them to stop crying."

Claire grimaced. "This isn't something we can handle over the phone."

"I didn't think so."

"I'll be right over."

By the time Claire drove up in front of the Brewster mansion, it was already nine o'clock. Loyalty to Norm had Claire feeling guilty for visiting her parents and doing her grocery shopping rather than staying home waiting for a call just like this one. But, to be honest, Evan and his brothers had seemed so determined that Claire genuinely believed they'd rather sign a pact with the devil than call someone for help.

Swallowing their pride and admitting their shortcomings in favor of the babies' needs had quickly, easily raised her opinion of them. But the Brewsters had actually elevated their reputations in her eyes by

how protective they were of their new brother and
sisters. Regardless of the fact that the babies were the
product of a marriage they didn't condone, the Brewster brothers had accepted the triplets without question
or qualm.

Even if they didn't have a clue how to care for
them.

She stepped out of her car and pulled out the box
of disposable diapers she'd picked up at the discount
store on her way to the Brewster estate. Studying the
two-story Tudor-style home, she walked to the front
door. Graceful touches of carved wood and stained
glass made the mansion the most lush, sophisticated
home Claire had ever seen.

Before she rang the bell, the door opened.

"Thank God! Come in! Come in!"

Taking the disposable diapers from her hands, Evan
dragged her into the elegant marble-and-cherry-wood
foyer. The chandelier sparkled radiantly, giving the
entry an unnaturally bright glow.

"Where are they?" she asked simply.

"Upstairs. Follow me."

Having changed from his suit into jeans and a T-
shirt, Evan looked even more attractive than he had
that morning at Arnie's office. His informal clothes
defined muscles hidden by his conservative black suit.
Once again, Claire had to remind herself that this gorgeous man was her boss. She occupied her mind by
studying the dark wood paneling as he led her up the
winding stairway to the landing and down the hall,
then opened the door to a huge, airy, colorful nursery.

"Oh," she breathed, first in sympathy for the kids,
who had cried so hard and so long they looked exhausted, then in appreciation of the beautiful room

with hardwood floors and wood trim and walls decorated in a rainbow motif.

Also dressed in jeans and T-shirts, Grant and Chas sat in two of the three rockers, clumsily holding the girls. Behind them were three identical cribs and behind the cribs were three uncurtained windows trimmed in the same oak as the rockers.

"Where's Cody?"

"Cody's in a round thing," Evan said as if that explained everything.

"A round thing?" Claire echoed, confused.

"I found some round thing with wheels that's got a seat in the middle. When I first put him in, he stopped crying and started sort of walking around, but that only lasted about twenty minutes, then he was howling with the girls again."

"Okay," Claire said, recognizing Evan had put Cody in a walker.

"You get Cody," she said. "And sit in the third rocker. For now, we'll just run through some of the basics."

Nodding obediently, Evan slipped around Chas's rocker and lifted Cody from the walker. Claire noticed all three kids wore pajamas and decided that was a step in the right direction—as long as they'd figured out how to tighten Cody's diaper.

"The first thing you need to know is that babies like to feel secure. So check the way you're holding your child. Make sure the baby can tell that you're not going to drop him or her."

Evan tossed her a completely exasperated look. "These kids need sleep."

"And they also need love, attention and affection," Claire said angrily, marching over and arranging

Evan's arms around Cody in such a way that the baby
would feel both protected and loved. The second her
hand made contact with his forearm, though, he
started as if she'd given him an electrical shock. Their
eyes met briefly, then both quickly looked away.

"Whether you guys understand this or not, you're
complete strangers to these babies," she continued as
she moved to Chas and manipulated his arms around
the baby he was holding. "They have to get to know
you or they won't sleep. They probably won't even
stop crying," she said, jerking Grant's arms until she
had them folded properly around the little girl. "In
fact, I'm going to suggest that each of you take a
child, one child, and be responsible for that child's
care, so that baby gets a sense of being special, being
important and feeling secure."

When all three kids were properly positioned, she
stepped back. "Now, keeping your hands and arms
around the baby just like I fixed them, bring the baby
up to your chest and cuddle her or him."

All three of the Brewster brothers did as they were
instructed.

"When you cuddle a baby," Claire continued,
"rub your cheek against the baby's cheek and whisper
soft things. Just tell her that you love her."

"This is weird…" Grant began, but Claire silenced
him with a look.

"These kids have been with strangers for the past
two days, and," she added softly, "they lost *their*
daddy, too. And their mom. What each one of them
needs right now more than anything else is a little bit
of love."

Crossing her arms on her chest as if daring them to
disagree, Claire watched all three shrewdly as—after

casting surreptitious glances at one another—each Brewster cuddled his child. As she'd instructed, they rubbed their cheeks on the babies' cheeks, they whispered endearments.

"Pat their backs," Claire encouraged quietly, because the sleepy children were calmer now.

"When was the last time you fed them?"

"We gave Taylor the final bottle right before Evan called you," Chas whispered. Though the little girl he held still sniffed and hiccuped, her crying had stopped and her swollen eyes were closed.

Claire swallowed the lump that formed in her throat. She could feel every iota of these babies' pain. She missed Norm, too. But on top of that, these kids were lonely and afraid, with strange people for the second time in only two days. "Have the other two eaten?" she asked, her voice soft and tender.

Evan nodded. "Everybody has had a bottle in the past hour."

"Then they're ready for bed," Claire whispered, motioning to indicate that all three children were breathing deeply and evenly. "But putting them into a crib is a very tricky thing, so we're going to do this one baby at a time."

The brothers nodded.

"Grant, you first. Stand up slowly," Claire said, walking over to the first crib. When Grant joined her, she said, "Bend at the waist so that your baby doesn't leave the warmth of your body until she's almost at the mattress."

Though his moves were awkward, Grant did exactly as he was told.

"Gently place the baby on the mattress and slide

your hand out from under her carefully...and slowly, so you don't disturb her.''

As if disarming a homemade bomb, Grant slowly, cautiously slid his hands out from under Annie. Claire motioned for him to take a few steps back, and he did. The baby continued to sleep. Grant sagged with relief.

Next, Claire motioned for Chas to do the same thing. She quietly repeated the instructions, and, as Grant had, Chas also went limp with relief.

Before Claire could motion to Evan, he was already on his way to the last crib. Without any direction from her, he laid Cody on the soft mattress, eased his hands and arms from under the child, stepped away, and then breathed a huge sigh of relief.

Claire had an odd intuition about the way Evan didn't wait for her help, almost as if he didn't want to risk her touching him again. Deciding she was putting too much meaning on things that probably had none, she clicked on the baby monitor and motioned for all three men to come out of the nursery. One by one they filed out into the hall. Claire gently closed the door behind them. Placing one finger on her lips, she cautioned them not to say anything and then directed them downstairs.

All four tiptoed down the circular stairway, through the foyer and into the all-white kitchen at the rear of the house. Collapsing on the stools in front of the counter, the brothers groaned.

"Parenting's not exactly as easy as it looks," Claire said with a laugh.

"How the hell do you know so much about kids?" Grant asked incredulously.

"She's got six brothers and sisters," Evan replied

before Claire could. Though she realized he knew the answer because she'd told him as much that afternoon, she felt a strange jolt of joy that he not only remembered but took the liberty of answering for her as if they were longtime friends.

"You're kidding," Grant gasped.

"Nope," Claire said, then walked to the counter to inspect the empty bottles. Again, she told herself not to make a mountain out of a molehill. She knew what was happening. She found Evan attractive and she wanted to think he found her attractive, too, so she was grasping for straws. "My youngest brother is six. Started first grade this year. Cute as a bug."

"But you don't live at home. Your phone number is listed under your name, not your parents', and I recognize that address as being part of a house converted into apartments," Evan observed, getting comfortable on his chair.

"I've been on my own since college," Claire informed him casually as she inspected the contents of the cupboards. Her heart had speeded up when she realized he not only remembered everything she told him but now knew where she lived.

But she stilled her thumping heart by reminding herself that he'd called her because he'd needed to get care for the babies. Then she told herself that even if he was attracted to her and she was to him, neither one of them could act on that attraction. First, he was her boss. Second, they had a ten-year age difference. Third, he was rich and she was poor. Dirt poor. Talk about nothing in common...

As she had hoped, she found baby food, formula and vitamins. She pulled out all three and set them on the counter. "It would have been hard for me to move back in with my family after college, but, also, my being home would have disrupted them. David was only about a year old when I left for school. He doesn't remember me being home. Kelly doesn't want to give up half her bedroom.'' She shrugged carelessly. "Having my own apartment suits everyone."

"You didn't move out because you hate kids?" Evan asked watchfully.

Claire laughed. "Heavens, no. I *love* kids."

All three men visibly relaxed.

"And I'll help you," she said with another lilting laugh. "Look here. These are prescription vitamins. Do you know what they tell you?"

"Yeah, that the kids don't eat right," Chas said, frowning.

"No, that the kids go to a pediatrician," Claire contradicted. "And see," she added, showing the men the label. "Right here is their pediatrician's name."

"Ah," Chas said happily. "That's good."

"That is good," Claire agreed. "Just by reading this label you'll know the dosage to give them, and the doctor to call to find out where they are with their immunizations."

"Immunizations?" Evan echoed, narrowing his eyes at Claire. "What the hell are you talking about?"

"Remember I told you that I was going to hit the basics with you?" Claire asked sweetly.

They nodded.

"Well, somebody get a notebook, because I think you're going to want to be writing some of this down."

"Okay," Grant said, rising from his seat. "I'll take charge of that."

"Splitting up everything is a good idea," Claire

said, while Grant rummaged for a pencil and paper. "I meant what I said upstairs about each of you taking a child. More than anything else, a baby needs a sense of security. If each of you more or less adopts one child as his own, each baby will get that sense of security."

Or things could actually fall apart, Evan thought, studying her carefully. He knew he didn't trust her because he suspected she was involved in Arnie's scheme to take the kids. He also believed that by bringing her into their home, he and his brothers had opened the door for her to continue aiding Arnie.

He knew his brothers didn't agree with him and thought he was being paranoid. But he also realized that he had more to lose than his brothers did. They might love these children in a generic way that mixed responsibility and a sense of family, but if something happened and they lost custody, Grant and Chas would get on with the rest of their lives. For Evan much, much more was at stake, because raising these children was his only chance at being a father.

"How did it go after I left last night?"

Though the question was perfectly innocent, Evan turned and glared at Claire. The insides of his eyelids felt like sandpaper, he was so tired he could have dropped where he stood, and his head hurt.

Between the cuddling and crooning, feeding and changing, Evan figured he'd gotten about two and a half hours' sleep. And since all three brothers awakened for every baby incident, he knew Chas and Grant hadn't fared any better than he had. But because the triplets couldn't be left alone, Chas and Grant got to stay home while Evan set off to handle the second

half of their responsibility, running the local lumber
mill.

"Kids wake up much?"

Another innocent question. Another narrowing of
Evan's eyes.

"My head hurts. I desperately need sleep. I never
realized how difficult it is to care for babies."

"Oh, come on," Claire said, following Evan into
his father's old office. "Babies are great. And believe
it or not, this is a wonderful stage in their lives...
except for the teething, but we'll cross that bridge
when we come to it."

Evan fell into his father's chair. "Teething. How
delightful."

"Trust me," Claire insisted, sitting on the corner
of the desk as if it was an old habit. "You're going
to love this."

Evan's gaze trailed from the curve of her buttocks
on the corner of the mahogany desk, down the line of
her thighs to the length of leg that currently dangled
over the side of his father's desk. She wore a chaste
navy-blue suit, the skirt loose and sufficiently long,
the blazer buttoned. She obviously wasn't trying to
draw attention to herself, but because he wasn't at his
professional best from lack of sleep, Evan found himself staring. Claire was a stunning woman, a naturally
beautiful woman with glossy black hair, eyes as wide
and as blue as the summer sky, and absolutely perfect
legs.

When she saw him looking at her legs, she quickly
jumped down and maneuvered herself into the chair
across from the desk. As if her movements finally
brought him completely awake, he realized he wanted

the truth about her and he wanted it now. He refused to work with someone he couldn't or didn't trust.

"I think you and I need to have a little talk."

In an unpretentious way she smiled at him, and Evan got a jolt of something that felt very much like attraction again, only this time laced with rightness. He wasn't merely attracted to this woman. He felt *drawn* to her. He sensed a sudden, overwhelming appropriateness about her being in his life, and he knew damned well that was foolish. Even if she wasn't a part of the Arnie Garrett scheme, he couldn't be involved with her. He couldn't be involved with *anyone*. He wouldn't tie a woman to a life without her own children, so there was no "right" woman for him.

"Three things happened yesterday," he said, steepling his fingers at his chin. "We buried my father and stepmother, my siblings and I inherited almost half of everything in this county, and I became a parent."

This time Claire raised her eyebrows. Without as much as a word from her, he knew she wanted to contradict him about "who" had become parents. He also knew that when the time was right, she wouldn't hesitate to correct him.

Evan swallowed—and not because she'd caught that inadvertent slip. The very fact that she had caught him, and wouldn't be afraid to tell him so, and the way she was absolutely comfortable in the chair across from him once again made it seem more than fitting that she was not only here in this office, but here in his life. And that bothered him. He could understand being attracted to her—any man over the age of twelve would be attracted to her—but the little jolts of rightness had to be a mistake of some sort.

Determined to ignore them, he cleared his throat. "Do you realize you were there for all three things?"

"Yes. I worked very closely with your father."

"Very closely," he agreed with a nod, glad she'd given him an opening to get to the topic that kept getting blotted out by chemistry or sexual awareness or some other damned male-female thing Evan didn't have time to deal with. "So close that I'd wager you know this business inside and out. *And* you know how to care for kids. Logically, Ms. Wilson, my brothers and I can't survive without you."

"Sure you could," Claire protested casually. "You could hire a nanny or something."

"Really? Overnight? On this tiny, sparsely populated piece of the mountain? I don't think so, and neither do you."

At the abrupt hardening of the expression in his eyes, Claire shifted uneasily on her seat. She didn't know what the heck he was driving at, but she had more than a sneaking suspicion she wasn't going to like it.

"If I were Arnie Garrett and I were trying to coerce custody of the triplets, there is only one person in this world who could help me."

Claire felt her mouth fall open in surprise. "What?" she said before she could stop herself. "I hope you don't think that I had something to do with Arnie Garrett trying to get you to sign over custody of the triplets!"

"That's exactly what I think," Evan said coolly.

"How dare you!" she gasped, angry in a way she didn't believe she'd ever been angry before. Most of that outrage came from her loyalty to this man's father and what she knew Norm would want for his children. "Those babies need to be raised by family. I'd never condone them being raised by anyone but you and your brothers. I'd have gone in search of you and insisted you take them before I'd let Arnie Garrett or anybody else have them, if only because I know that's what your father wanted."

"That is what my father wanted," Evan agreed, waving her back down when Claire sprang from her chair as if to storm out of the room. "I apologize for questioning you, but I had to know whose side you were on."

"Who says there are sides?" she demanded, furious. "You're the only person I see making trouble. Everybody else seems perfectly happy with this situation."

"I don't agree with you. I don't think Arnie Garrett is happy with this situation. I don't think he's done trying for the kids. And *I* want the kids. If there's a war, Ms. Wilson, let me assure you I plan to win it."

"I don't doubt it," Claire agreed quietly. "But you keep talking about those kids as if they are exclusively yours and they're not. You have two brothers and the triplets need to be raised by all three of you, not just one of you."

"Grant owns a construction company in Savannah. Chas has an interview with a law firm in Philadelphia in a few weeks. But I could and did leave my job, and my life. Just like that," he said, snapping his fingers. "I'm here to stay. In the end, those kids will be raised by me. Probably exclusively. And nobody's going to keep me from doing that."

"You saw me as that much of a threat?" she asked.

Cool, dignified, he caught her gaze. "I didn't know what to think about you. That's why I decided to confront you. Now that I see how loyal to my father you are, I sincerely doubt you could help Arnie do something my father wouldn't have wanted."

Stupefied, Claire stared at him. He wore a gray suit, a white shirt and a moss-green tie that brought out the verdant color of his eyes. Those eyes held a determined spark, but his perfect mouth tipped upward, just a fraction, as if he was relieved and couldn't quite hide it. He looked innocent and sweet, and positively gorgeous. Not nervous. Not confused. Absolutely normal.

In a wave of understanding, she realized this conversation answered the question about why he behaved so oddly around her. He thought she was in cahoots with Arnie Garrett. He hadn't been getting the same peculiar sensations she'd been getting for the past two days.

Not only was her body constantly on red alert, but she continually experienced a strange intuition that they were made for each other. That wasn't just preposterous, it was premature. She didn't even know the man, for pete's sake. True, he was gorgeous, beautifully built and had a smile that could charm the angels, but it took much, much more than that to be "made for each other."

And now she knew he wasn't attracted to her. But, in fairness, she didn't *want* to be attracted to him either. She couldn't afford to be attracted to him. He was older. He was her boss. And he was way, way out of her social circle.

"It's been a really difficult two days for all of us," she said, though she wouldn't meet his eyes. She couldn't. Something completely wrong was happening to her, and unless or until she was sure she could manage it, she wasn't going to take any chances. "I have some things I need to do this morning. If you're going to pick up where your father left off, those contracts—" she pointed at the corner of his father's desk "—need to be renegotiated. I'd start there, if I were you."

Evan nodded. Claire let herself out of his office and closed the door, since her desk was right outside and she didn't want him watching her every move any more than she wanted to be reminded of him.

She didn't need privacy or time to think about this. Her mother's involvement with an older, more sophisticated...richer man had cost Claire her father.

Staying away from Evan Brewster should be a no-brainer.

Chapter Three

After work, Claire followed Evan to the Brewster mansion. Because she had been quiet all afternoon, Evan suspected she was probably still annoyed with him for suggesting she might have been in league with Arnie Garrett. For Evan that was good news and bad news. On the one hand, her irritation was a sort of proof that she hadn't thrown in her lot with Arnie and Evan could trust her. On the other, being able to trust her nullified the argument he continually used to pull himself away from noticing she was a woman. If she wasn't in partnership with Arnie to take the triplets, then there was no reason not to find her attractive. None, except that he had nothing to offer a wife, so he wasn't in the market.

And he wasn't. He had even begun to seriously doubt his attraction to her, in spite of the way it seemed to get worse as the day went on. Huddled together in two rooms, cocooned from the rest of the lumber mill, they were in their own private world. He was sure most of what he was feeling was nothing more than a response to being so close all the time.

As he pulled into the driveway, Evan wasn't concerned about having to spend extra hours with Claire, since nobody would have time to be attracted to anyone while trying to feed, bathe and put to bed three children. If anything, these next few hours would probably nip the attraction in the bud.

He waited for her by the front door while she parked her car. When she met him at the entryway, he smiled. "Are you sure you're ready for this?"

She laughed. It was the first time she'd laughed all day, and though Evan wished the sound hadn't pleased him so much, he took it as a sign that she'd forgiven him for mistrusting her.

"I said I didn't mind helping you guys get adjusted to parenting, and I don't," she said cheerily.

"You're sure?"

"Are you trying to get rid of me?"

Wondering if that wasn't exactly what he was trying to do, Evan opened the door. "Welcome to paradise."

Crying was the music that greeted them. Evan could see Grant running back and forth in the kitchen. A glance to the right showed Chas had all three sobbing kids corralled in the living room...on the white rug, white sofa and white wing chair.

"What are you doing?" he asked with a gasp, then strode in and scooped Cody off the rug. "Are you blind? Everything in here is white."

"The kids are clean," Chas argued in exasperation.

"Maybe now, but..."

Evan stopped when Claire tapped him on the shoulder. "I think I should go in the kitchen and help."

"Good thinking."

The minute Claire left the room, some of Evan's tension eased. He lowered himself to the sofa and settled Cody on his lap. "Sorry," he said to Chas. "I know you guys probably had a hell of a day."

"That's okay," Chas said, easily accepting his apology. "I imagine your day couldn't have been any easier than ours."

"Actually, my day wasn't too bad," Evan admitted, pressing his cheek against the top of Cody's head, not just because it was one of the little gestures of affection Claire had taught them the night before but because it felt right, good. Holding the baby was like getting grounded. Even amid the noise and confusion, everything they were going through made sense when Evan held one of the babies.

"Claire is very much on top of things," he continued. "She seems to have the entire sequence of events down. When a contract comes in, she knows how to schedule inventory, labor and delivery, and then how to put each contract into the accounting system so it gets billed."

"That's a relief," Chas said as he successfully caught Taylor, who was crawling away as if drag racing with Annie. Unfortunately, he just missed Annie, who eluded him by scrambling around the leg of the coffee table.

Today the girls wore ruffly yellow dresses with a row of very happy daisies across the front hem. Annie, who was now playing peekaboo with Chas around the leg of the table, was so cute Evan was momentarily taken aback. Sometimes when he looked at the kids and realized they were his to raise, he felt the overwhelming sensation that he was in the middle of a miracle.

He reached out and grabbed the ruffled rump of Annie's tights as she tried to climb on the coffee table.

Chas nodded appreciatively. "So we're set, then," he confirmed.

"We're set," Evan agreed.

"As long as we keep Claire," Chas reminded his brother with a note of warning in his voice.

"I'm not going to do anything rash," Evan said. Realizing it wouldn't be wise to tell his brother he'd accused Claire of being in league with Arnie, Evan stayed silent. He didn't even confide that it bothered him to be so dependent on another person, because they didn't have a choice. Claire knew how to care for babies. She knew how to run the family business. Right at this moment, they needed her for both. Until he and his brothers learned how to care for the kids and run the mill, they couldn't live without her.

He said a silent prayer that he was smart enough not to take his attraction seriously. Even if he discounted his three main concerns—her age, the fact that he was her boss and she was his employee, and the fact that he had nothing to offer her—being so dependent made it much too risky to be attracted to her. If he made a pass at her and she rebuffed him, or worse, if they started a relationship that fizzled, the entire Brewster family would be up the creek without a paddle.

"All you have to do is be nice to her," Evan whispered to himself as he got off the small elevator. Admitting how dependent his family was on Claire, and recognizing how close he'd come to alienating her the day before, he knew he had to behave himself. He couldn't yell at her or accuse her of things anymore. He couldn't be attracted to her. He had to find the middle of the road.

He pushed open the door to Claire's office and she turned from a filing cabinet and smiled. "Hi."

Evan's breath froze in his lungs. Her clinging powder-blue knit dress outlined every delicious curve of her body, accented her brilliant sapphire eyes and brought each of Evan's nerve endings to complete attention. He reminded himself of all the good reasons he had to stomp this attraction out as if it were a used cigarette, but in the end only the thought of losing the children brought him in line. He silently cursed himself for being weak, but decided it was surprise that had tricked him into reacting. Tomorrow morning he'd be prepared for the fact that she'd be gorgeous in a gunnysack, and he wouldn't react.

And it wasn't too late to save himself today. He might have reacted, but she didn't seem to have noticed. He could still pull this one out of the fire.

"Good morning," Evan said, taking her friendly greeting and reducing it to a pleasantry between co-workers. Without another word, he strode to the door of his office.

"Do you want me to come in with you?" Claire asked politely. "We could look at the mail."

Evan stopped. He considered that he had two options. One, make up an excuse that would give his breathing a little time to get back to normal and his libido the opportunity to do the same. Or two, he could simply bite the bullet, let her come into his office and force himself to stay in line.

Two was the right thing. But one was the smart thing. "Give me a few minutes to get settled."

"Okay."

Evan tossed his briefcase onto a convenient chair and strode to his desk, where he began organizing the papers he'd reviewed the day before. He heard the sound of the elevator, heard a man greet Claire, and waited for her to announce the visitor. Instead, the sound of laughter from the other room drifted through the air.

His first reaction was a swift stab of jealousy, but he talked himself out of it easily. Claire was a happy person. It would surprise him if she *didn't* get along well with the staff.

When laughter continued to float into his office for the next five minutes, Evan changed his mind about being calm and he rose. He wasn't jealous, he assured himself. He wasn't concerned that a man had arrived just to visit Claire, either. She had a right to speak with whomever she wanted. The problem was, he suddenly, fervently wished it was him. She was funny, sensitive, smart. And sassy. The sassy part really got to him because he liked the fact that she wasn't afraid to stand up to him and his brothers. If she were older, he wouldn't worry about his not being able to have children. He'd ask her out and let the chips fall where they may…that is, if she didn't work for him.

That thought caused him to sit again and ponder the possibilities. It wasn't that he didn't have any work to do, but this was much more fun than thinking about easements, rights-of-way and prices for lumber. He would definitely ask her out if she were older and just a woman he'd met on the street. Her sassiness proved that she could take care of herself, that she was able to think things through and come to conclusions she would defend. So, if she were older—and just a woman he'd met on the street—he'd roll the dice, and let her make the choices.

The problem was, she wasn't older.

And she did work for him.

"I think we need to give your brothers a break."

Evan looked up from the paperwork he was reviewing in the den. Taylor sat on his lap, playing pattycake with his chest, his desk and herself, but after a week Evan had become accustomed to working, eating and watching television with a child on his lap and he didn't even notice her.

"What kind of a break?"

"They've been cooped up in the house with the kids for six days. Neither one has even gone out in the yard without one of the kids. You and I both get free time at the office, but Chas and Grant have been stuck here twenty-four hours a day."

Whether he wanted to admit it or not, Evan knew Claire was right. But he didn't like the odd, unsettling feeling he got thinking about spending an entire evening alone with her, with only three babies as chaperons. It wasn't that he didn't trust himself, but he didn't want to risk his fantasies getting any more intimate, any more detailed than they already were. Though he had controled himself outwardly over the past week, in his mind he kept imagining how different things would be if she were older, or just a woman he'd met on the street....

Damn it. He was doing it again.

"What do you suggest?" he asked, leaning back on his chair. "That we send them to a bar?"

"It couldn't hurt."

"Obviously, you haven't heard much about our last night in this town two years ago."

"You're right," Claire said, walking into the den and taking a seat in front of the desk. She'd begun bringing an extra set of clothes to work for the evening, and she wore natural-fit jeans and a brightly printed blouse. The dark colors of the blouse made her skin glow, even as they caught the blue of her eyes and enhanced it. "I haven't heard a lot, only rumors and innuendo. Want to clue me in?"

Evan grimaced, realizing that in life you always got your due, because the reputation that had seemed to enhance his appeal to the women of his youth would undoubtedly have exactly the opposite effect on this woman. Nonetheless, he had the strangest urge to get this out in the open, to have her know the truth and trust him, anyway. "You'll hate us."

"I doubt it," Claire disagreed. "What could you have done that would be so bad?"

"Grant went through the big window at Potter's."

"Ouch," Claire said, but she laughed. "At least *he* went through it and didn't throw somebody else through."

"No, he did that at Montgomery's."

"That's what this town gets for having two bars."

"And a social club. Let's not forget the social club."

"What did you do there?" Claire asked with a laugh, feeling an avalanche of emotions. After a week of him virtually ignoring her, she was inordinately happy he finally seemed willing to be personal with her the way his two brothers had been all along. She was beginning to think Evan was so private she'd never have a normal relationship with him. But here they were, talking easily about subjects Norm considered taboo. It was either proof that Evan had grown beyond the episodes enough that he could laugh about them, or proof that he trusted her—which was such a relief she could have collapsed against her chair.

"After we bought several rounds of drinks for everyone, we picked up and left."

Puzzled, Claire stared at him. He had the most wonderful face. His skin was marred only by a slight shadow from a day's growth of beard, but that actually augmented his already good looks. His clear green eyes held a twinkle of amusement. His full, wonderful lips had bowed into a smile.

If he wasn't her boss, and if she wasn't struggling for both dignity and decorum as a way to prove herself to him since she wasn't quite sure that she had, she would have sighed with appreciation. Instead, she said, "That doesn't sound so bad."

"It wasn't. I only told you that to show you that we weren't completely corrupt."

"You don't have to tell me that. I'd already figured that out on my own."

And she didn't care to explain why or how. She suspected he already knew she found him irresistibly sweet with the kids and incredibly attractive. He didn't need to know she was beginning to see he and his brothers had grown up and become strong, sensitive men. Then he'd realize her attraction to him was edging into some very dangerous territory.

She left the room and went looking for Grant and Chas. When she found them, she sent them into the den with Evan. When they whooped with joy after only about thirty seconds, Claire assumed Evan had suggested they have a night out. Twenty minutes later, kneeling beside the tub as the triplets splashed water at one another, she heard the sound of tires squealing and gravel flying and knew the Brewster brothers were on their way into town. She closed her eyes and said a silent prayer for the virtue of the local girls. When she opened them, Evan was beside her.

"Getting tired?" he asked guiltily.

She shook her head and smiled. "No, just sending a suggestion or two to the man upstairs."

"You were praying for my brothers?"

"No. I was praying for the local girls."

Evan burst out laughing. "You have heard some tales, haven't you?" he asked, sitting on the rim of the tub and dividing his attention between splashing with the kids and talking with Claire.

"Only enough to scare me witless the day I met you."

"Regardless of what's fact and what's fantasy, we've all changed," Evan said seriously. "Even before we came home, all three of us had settled down. Grant actually owns a highly successful construction company down south. Chas is waiting for his results from the bar exam."

"And you were third person from the top at a company that buys and manages fast-food franchises."

Evan raised his eyebrows as if impressed by her knowledge.

"You weren't going to tell me that, were you?"

"I don't brag."

"But you owned part of that company. You're independently wealthy. You don't need the lumber mill."

Evan dismissed her remark. "Neither does Grant," he said, splashing Cody, who giggled in response.

"So, why are you guys staying?"

He thought about that for a minute. "Family pride, tradition, loyalty." He paused, caught her gaze. "Plus, there's no better place to raise kids. I have three, you know."

They stared into each other's eyes for several seconds and Claire had the distinct impression he was warning her off. This was more than their running disagreement about each brother taking a child under his wing. This was a personal caution, as if he was reminding her that he was a package deal. If she wanted him, she got three kids, too.

It embarrassed her to realize he understood just how attractive she found him, then she downplayed it. He probably had hundreds of women who were attracted to him. She didn't need to be embarrassed, only to realize she was normal and get herself in line, as he was warning her to do.

"And I'm sure you're going to do a terrific job," she said as she grabbed a towel and pulled Annie from the tub. As a reward for the service, Annie placed two wet hands on Claire's cheeks. "In another couple of weeks, you guys won't need me anymore. The three of you will turn into fabulous fathers." She rubbed noses with Annie. But another thought struck, and she risked catching Evan's gaze again. "But kids still need a mother," she advised softly. "No matter how good you get at being a father, these kids still need a mother. Since you're thirty-three and not married, I suspect you're more than a little selective in the mate department. And I guess what I'm telling you is that you might want to change your standards."

Evan thought about what Claire had told him. Actually, it haunted him. She was right. The kids needed a female in their lives. She was also right in thinking he was selective. He had to be. Since he couldn't have children, he couldn't offer a woman the things a normal man could offer.

But now that he had the triplets, everything had changed. He couldn't offer a woman the chance to have her own children, but he could offer her children—a family. He still had to be careful, but at least now he had parameters, guidelines. A place to start.

"Good morning," he said as he strode off the elevator and into Claire's office. Her peach suit brought out the richness of her dark hair and the beauty of her skin. He swallowed hard, remembering all the things he'd deduced the night before, including the fact that Claire couldn't be the woman he chose to be the mother of his triplets. If they started a relationship and she grew to love him, Claire might accept not having children of her own, but the truth was, no one but his father knew he couldn't have kids and Evan couldn't disclose his secret until he was sure of the relationship. By then she'd be in deep enough that if she made the opposite choice, she'd end up hurt. She was too young to be put in that kind of position, too young to sign away her right to her own children.

"Good morning, Evan," she answered pleasantly, smiling at him.

Evan felt a tug of regret, but reminded himself his attraction to her, at this point, was mostly physical. And since she didn't really know him, she also could have no attraction to him beyond a physical one. If they behaved themselves now, neither one of them needed to get hurt.

"Are you ready to go through the mail?"

"Not really." He needed a minute. His logic might be sound, his intentions might be good, but he was still human.

"Can I have a few minutes?"

"Five?"

That stopped him. She was doing it again. In the past week, not only had she dictated his jobs and tasks, and circumvented him whenever possible in the day-to-day operations of the mill, but she continually tried to set his schedule.

He frowned and turned to look at her. "How about if I buzz you when I'm ready?"

"Okay, fine," she said, but she looked disappointed. "I'm sure I can find something to do until you're ready."

"Don't you have anything to do?"

Claire laughed. "I have plenty to do. But I don't want to get started on something, only to have to put it down when you buzz me." She waved her hand in dismissal. "Go. I'm fine. I'll find something to do."

Oddly uncomfortable, Evan walked to his desk. He pulled his copy of the *Wall Street Journal* out of his briefcase and opened it to the previous day's stock results.

Before two minutes had passed, his office door opened and Claire entered carrying a steaming mug of coffee. "I thought you might like this," she said cheerfully as she set the mug on his desk, then she saw the paper. "Oh, does this mean you're ready for me?"

"No," Evan replied evenly, though his emotions continued to duke it out for control. Part of him was still experiencing extreme responses to how good she looked. The other part, the businessman, didn't like her tone. "This means I'm easing myself into the day after a difficult night with three babies." He sent her a level look. "Thank you for the coffee. I'll buzz you when I'm ready."

She visibly bristled. "Okay."

Evan allowed himself twenty long minutes to read the paper and sip his coffee. He deliberately dragged his feet because his anger with her could quickly be overpowered by his attraction to her. And he didn't want to say something foolish. Since he couldn't risk his real reaction, he had to make sure she got his subtle message about planning his day for him. After he got accustomed to how pretty she was, his employee-employer relations would be handled a little more professionally, but after a night with very little sleep, Evan figured he was lucky to be able to have thought this far ahead.

He pushed the intercom button on his phone and dialed her number. She answered on the third ring. "I'm ready to go over anything you want to go over."

For a good ten seconds there was no answer, then

she said, "Actually, I'm right in the middle of something and I can't stop."

He didn't have a clue what that might be, but given that discretion was the better part of valor, he simply said, "How about if I check back with you in twenty minutes?"

"No. It would probably be better if I called you when I was done."

"Do you think it's going to take longer than twenty minutes to finish your task?"

"No."

"Then it shouldn't be a problem for you to wait for me to call you back."

Evan hung up the phone with a satisfied smirk, but his smile quickly faded because he felt childish. He didn't need to resort to stupid tricks like this to feel he was in command. In fact, he decided to go out to her office on the pretense of getting another cup of coffee and tell her to simply call him when she was ready.

Glad to feel like a mature adult again, Evan opened the door that separated their offices. When he saw that she was reading *Cosmopolitan*, his eyes narrowed with fury. "What are you doing?" he asked in a deadly quiet voice.

She jumped a foot in the air. "Oh my gosh, you scared me."

"I should be firing you. You're reading a magazine on company time, and after I called you in to do some work with me!"

"Well, I asked you to do some work with me and you pulled out the *Wall Street Journal*."

"I own this business. If I want to read a paper, I'm

allowed, but more than that, did it ever occur to you that I was researching investments for the company?"

"You might have been, but you could have done that anytime. I have work that needs to be attended to *now*."

Her audacity stunned him, and all he could do was stare at her. Knowing there was no easy or polite way out of this argument, he turned to walk into his office and said, "Then let's see this amazingly important work of yours. Lord knows we wouldn't want it to sit for ten minutes."

He strode to his desk without another word, convinced that she'd won a battle with her ploy, but also convinced that if he hadn't given her the victory, he would have been behaving even more childishly. When she actually began discussing the open projects for which she needed answers, as well as the mail from the day before, Evan began to sink down into his chair.

She really had needed him, and he'd ignored her because he was afraid his reactions to her were becoming too obvious.

When she was through with her questions, she politely rose from her chair. "Thank you for your help."

He swallowed. "You're welcome."

Then she walked out of his office, her head held high, her sweet little bottom swaying ever so slightly. When she closed the door, Evan hung his head and groaned. *What in the hell was happening to him?*

The next day Evan realized he knew what was happening to him. He was overwhelmed with the responsibility of the company and three babies. He was attracted to a woman he couldn't have. And he was letting his emotions dominate him.

So he made some decisions. He *needed* to find a wife. He hadn't had a relationship in three years. It was no wonder the first beautiful woman to come along was his undoing. He needed a mother for the kids, he needed a mate, he needed a companion, and—just like any normal man—he needed sex.

Though he believed that would solve most of his problems, Evan was nothing if not pragmatic. He knew Claire had also overstepped her boundaries the day before. He wasn't sure how much liberty his father had given her, but Evan found it hard to believe Norm Brewster had let her rule him, the office and the company. Like it or not, Evan had to settle this matter.

Since the office was her turf, she was completely comfortable and in control. Evan, however, was an outsider, an interloper, and sometimes that's how she made him feel. So he concluded the best way to get them on the right footing again was to take her out of the office and onto neutral ground.

At twelve, he walked into her office and waited for her to look up from her computer and acknowledge him.

"How about lunch?" he asked quietly.

"I brown-bagged it today."

"So, save it. I'm in the mood to go to the diner. I'll buy," he added.

He could see by the expression on her face that she didn't trust this, but she politely accepted his invitation and rose from her seat. They walked to the parking lot in silence, got into his Explorer and drove the five miles into town in a silence broken only by fleeting comments on the weather, the beauty of the trees this year, and one short story about the babies.

The second they took seats in the booth, she confronted him. "You want to yell at me, don't you?"

"No," he said, not even slightly surprised by her perception. "What I want to do is make a few things clear."

"That's just a fancy way of saying yell."

Evan shook his head. Had he said he liked her sass? "Claire, my family and I need you. On some levels I actually think we're taking advantage of you."

"That's not true," she said quietly. "I'm helping you because I want to. Because I really liked your father and appreciated everything he did for me. I didn't have many job prospects. Your father gave me a job when no one else wanted me."

"Really?" Evan said, curious, confused, but before he could question her further, their waitress arrived.

"Good morning, Claire," she said brightly.

"Hi, Abby," Claire replied. "This is Evan Brewster. Second oldest of Norm's kids, and my new boss."

"It's a pleasure to meet you, Mr. Brewster."

"Thank you. It's a pleasure to meet you, too." In a town as small as Brewster, everybody knew everybody else, but Abby wasn't merely a stunning redhead with huge green eyes, she was something of a celebrity, because her father had been mayor forever. She had also gotten pregnant in high school and had a son by Hunter Wyman who Abby's parents had run out of town. Because her family was wealthy, it puzzled Evan that she was working at the diner.

"Here are your menus," Abby said pleasantly. "I'll give you five minutes and come back for your orders."

"Thank you," Claire said.

"Thank you," Evan echoed, then immediately turned to Claire. "Doesn't her family own the bed-and-breakfast?"

"Actually, Abby owns it herself."

"I'm lost," Evan admitted. "She owns the bed-and-breakfast, her father is mayor, her family has significant holdings throughout the state. Why is she here?"

"I forgot you've been gone for two years," Claire said apologetically. "Her father died last year, but not before medical bills ate up just about everything they owned. Abby kept the bed-and-breakfast, but it doesn't make a lot of money now that the chain hotels have started popping up along the other turnpike exits."

"So, she's here."

"She doesn't mind," Claire put in carefully. "Funny how life changes, isn't it?"

Evan turned, studying Abby. "It's not funny. It's more like odd."

"You're telling me. Last year when I graduated I was struggling to find a job, then your father helped me, taught me a million things, gave me a great salary and a position in the community, and now he's gone."

"And I'm here in his place," Evan put in sympathetically. "But, Claire, that doesn't have to be bad. I've already acknowledged how much we need you, but I'm not going to pretend our getting adjusted to each other is going to be easy, either."

"Okay," Abby said, returning to their table. "Everybody ready to order?"

Evan smiled at her. "The daily soup and a salad and coffee."

"Okay," Abby said, scribbling the order.

"Same for me," Claire said, and, still scribbling, Abby nodded and turned away.

"She's such a lovely person," Claire remarked as Abby walked back to the kitchen of the diner.

"Yes, she is," Evan agreed, staring after her. What had happened to her was almost the exact opposite of what had happened to him. She'd inherited nothing and now struggled to keep her family together. He'd inherited more than he'd ever need and got a family, to boot. Life was so peculiar.

"And she's tough," Claire added. "You don't have to worry about her so much."

Evan grimaced. "Am I that obvious?"

"Evan, everything you think is usually written all over your face."

Evan felt that same readable face color uncontrollably. He hoped she didn't realize how attracted he was to her, because some of his thoughts hadn't exactly been pure. But he also hoped she couldn't see the rejection, either, because his reasons for rejecting her were not personal, or her fault.

"Salad," Abby said, setting two bowls in front of them and a basket of rolls. "Soup will be along in a minute. By the way," she said, facing Claire. "Tyler loved your birthday gift. He'll be sending you a thank you card."

Claire grinned. "I'll look forward to it. You tell

him that it has to be homemade and I want at least two pictures.''

Shaking her head as she chuckled, Abby walked away.

"Encouraging the local talent?" Evan asked curiously.

"Absolutely. I wouldn't be where I am if your father hadn't encouraged me, so I like to encourage anyone I can. But more than that, Abby's alone. She needs all the friends she can get. Tyler needs all the family he can get...."

Even as she said the words, Evan felt his mouth fall open. He glanced at Abby, considered his own situation, considered hers, and felt himself go numb with the realization that they were perfect for each other.

Chapter Four

Claire watched Evan's face as some sort of realization dawned on him, though she didn't have a clue what it was. Not comfortable in the continued silence, she said, "I thought you wanted to talk to me about something?"

At the sound of her words, he started, then turned to face her. "I'm sorry. I didn't hear what you said."

She almost said, "Obviously," but changed her mind and asked, "You brought me here to talk to me, didn't you?"

"Oh, yes. Yes," he said, then cleared his throat.

"I don't want to yell at you," he stated emphatically. "But I did want to make something clear, and I wanted to do it out of the office because I think you need some objectivity."

"*I* need some objectivity?" she asked incredulously, sure he had things backward.

"Here's the way I see this. You and my father ran the lumber mill for the past year. In that time, you grew in your understanding of the business and my father undoubtedly gave you more and more responsibility.''

Claire nodded.

"But now I'm taking over the mill and I sense— no, I know—that you have a better grasp of the business than I do.''

"And this is bad because…?'' Claire asked, getting annoyed. It almost sounded as if she was being criticized for doing her job well.

"Because I may not want to run the business the same way my father did.''

Claire knew he had a right to operate the business any way he wanted to. In fact, he had a responsibility to manage it the best way he knew how. "And my continuing with your father's practices is hindering you,'' she said blandly.

"No,'' Evan disagreed. "It's more or less shutting me out. If you try to keep the same schedule you had when my father was alive, doing things the way you always did them, I'm out of the loop because I don't know all the things you do.''

Claire blew her breath out on a long sigh. "You're right. I'm sorry.''

"There's nothing for you to be sorry about,'' Evan said, then he grimaced. "Well, maybe the bit with *Cosmopolitan* was pushing it, but otherwise, this isn't your fault. It's mine. I should have been more available.''

Claire nodded her agreement, seeing his point, willing to help and not even feeling chastised, as Abby returned with their check for lunch. Abby smiled at Evan, Evan smiled in return, and all Claire's good feelings instantly evaporated. She experienced a sud-

den pain that felt very much like a knife in the heart—
which was, she reminded herself, ridiculous.

"Do I pay for this here?" Evan asked Abby with
another warm smile.

Abby glowed under his approval. "How about if I
take it at the register?"

"Great," Evan said. "I'll be up in a minute."

It wasn't lost on Claire that he said, *I'll* be up in a
minute, but before the knife twisted, or before she
wallowed in misery at the knowledge that he was trying to get rid of her, she rose from her seat. "I think
I'll go out to the car and get a breath of fresh air while
you pay."

Outside she reminded herself again that she wasn't
interested in him romantically for many reasons. He
was older. He was her boss, and they were already
having problems working together without adding another complication. On top of all that, they came from
two different worlds.

But he didn't come from a different world from
Abby's, and their other complications were minimal,
as well. Though Claire and Abby were the same age,
Abby didn't work for Evan, and she was accustomed
to being one of the town's elite rather than the town's
waitress. Suddenly, Claire realized that Evan and
Abby were made for each other. Where dating someone like Evan would be a new experience for Claire,
for Abby, it would be normal.

But even more than that, after the horrendous years
Abby had recently had, she deserved a break. And
marrying a Brewster was certainly a break.

Evan returned to the car whistling. Claire smiled at
him, squelching the unwanted twinge of envy that
managed to squeeze through her very solid logic.

"When we get back to the office," she said, "how about if I create a list of all the things I do? This afternoon we can review it together."

"That would be great," Evan said, and hearing the happy tone in his voice, Claire knew not only that he was glad to have met Abby, but that her jealousy wouldn't do her any good.

Claire might have recognized jealousy wouldn't do her any good, but she couldn't stop the intuition or instincts that kept nagging at her, forcing her to draw conclusions that were supposed to be wrong. She knew all the reasons why it was inappropriate for her and Evan to be involved. She knew all the reasons why it was good for him to be involved with Abby. She even wished him a good time when he left for every one of the dates he had with Abby in the two weeks that followed. But one Sunday afternoon, sitting under a huge oak tree, reading as the kids crawled and played in a fenced-in area of the yard, Claire felt a stab of rightness so consuming it took her breath away.

As she watched Evan rolling a ball to the children and encouraging them to roll it back, she knew what bothered her the most about this. He wasn't like the man she'd expected a wealthy, successful, handsome Brewster to be. He was absolutely normal. He wasn't vain, arrogant, self-important, self-interested or even driven. He was a hard worker, but he made time for the kids. He loved the kids. He was loyal to a fault with his brothers. He didn't put much stock in power and position...and, damn it, he was so attracted to her he couldn't hide it!

She'd seen him peeking at her, staring at her and even out and out daydreaming about her, if the expression on his face was anything to go by. He wanted to kiss her because he liked her, and she liked him. They laughed at the same jokes, ate the same food, adored these triplets... He even seemed to admire her when she stood up to him.

Yet he was dating Abby, and Claire was afraid her best friend was going to get hurt, or worse yet, that Evan was somehow using her....

Chas walked out the back door, across the patio to the picnic table where Claire sat. "Are you sure you don't mind that Grant and I have another night out?"

"Hey, I went out Friday night." With her friends, but Claire wasn't about to tell them that. Let them all think she had a date. "Evan went out last night. It's your turn."

"Great, thanks," Chas said, then impulsively took her face in his hands and kissed her forehead. "You're a doll."

Evan watched the episode silently, then, with narrowed eyes, followed Chas's walk back into the house.

"You have a problem with Chas kissing my forehead?"

Evan took a deep breath. "Yes and no," he confessed quietly, and Claire's heart constricted. After all her confusion, it seemed they were at a moment of truth. If he admitted he liked her more than as a friend, she would admit she liked him, too, and was ready to let the chips fall where they may.

"Because...?" she urged softly.

"Because, Claire, damn it, you work for us and we need you. I don't want Chas breaking your heart or some other damned thing and then having you...well, hurt."

Stung, irritated, Claire only stared at his back as he paced away from her.

"I see."

"What did you want me to say?" Evan demanded, spinning to face her. "Did you want me to say I find you attractive and I don't want Chas anywhere near you?"

She nearly said yes, but changed her mind. In the past two weeks she'd seen Evan was proud and stubborn to a fault. That was why he'd stayed away from his father for so long, even though he obviously adored the man.

"I never said a word about your being jealous. I never mentioned that you might find me attractive. You brought it up. You deal with it." With that she rose from the picnic table. "I'm going to start the kids' dinner."

When he came into the house twenty minutes later, Evan apologized. Running his hand along the back of his neck, he said, "I shouldn't have said that."

"If it was the truth, I think you should have."

He only grunted a response, settling Annie and Taylor in separate high chairs and stalking outside to get Cody. Frowning, Claire stared after him. He might have been avoiding her initially because he disliked the fact that they worked together, but since they were both sensible and mature, that really shouldn't bother him. He couldn't dislike the fact that she was ten years younger than he was because Abby was the same—unless Abby had something Claire didn't have?

The next morning Claire decided she'd imagined everything. Evan's demeanor toward her was professional and polite, and he was abundantly pleasant. So when she caught him staring at her as she filed some folders in a cabinet in front of his office, she concluded he was so engrossed in his thoughts he didn't know where his eyes were. When their hands brushed because both reached for the same paper and she got a jolt of electricity that nearly buckled her knees, she didn't even look to see if he'd had a reaction because she knew he hadn't.

But when they were washing dishes that night, Claire started having serious second thoughts. He wouldn't touch her, hardly looked at her, and hadn't said two words since they'd arrived at his home. If he wasn't fighting an attraction, then something was bothering him. And, frankly, she believed she had earned a right to know what it was.

"You're awfully quiet," she observed boldly.

"I'm tired."

Grabbing a dish to dry, she flippantly asked, "Have a date tonight?"

"No."

"Well then, I guess it doesn't matter that you're tired."

"No, I guess it doesn't." He turned away from her, and Claire decided she'd done enough pushing for one night. She didn't know why she had pushed at all, except that she was starting to think she was crazy. One minute she was sure he was attracted to her. The next, his behavior had her convinced he wasn't. It almost appeared as if some perverse side of her wanted to force him into making an unequivocal declaration. Since that was the crazy part, Claire moved away from the sink to store a pot across the room.

Certain that she was the one with the problem, she

was flabbergasted when she spun away from the cupboard and nearly bumped into Evan. He caught her by the elbows to steady her, and Claire got the sparks, goose bumps and shivers of awareness she always got when he was within ten feet. This time, however, her gaze lifted to his before he had a chance to deny or disguise his reaction. His eyes narrowed, and almost immediately turned a hazy, sexy green. He drew in a sharp breath.

Their bodies were nearly pressed together. His hands clutched her elbows. If either one of them moved six inches, their noses would be brushing.

"Sorry," he whispered hoarsely, then his eyes lowered and focused on her mouth. In response, Claire licked her suddenly dry lips. Evan swallowed hard.

"I'm sorry, too," she croaked, wishing—almost willing—him to kiss her. Damn it, she was attracted to him. He was attracted to her. What the hell was the problem?

When he stepped away, pivoted in the other direction and strode to the sink, Claire sagged in defeat.

"I was thinking about your suggestion that each of us take a child and more or less raise that child as our own."

"That wasn't precisely what I said," Claire told him, still dazed from her brush with reality and now confused by his abrupt attempt at conversation. "But I guess it's close enough."

"Well, I've been thinking about it and I've decided it doesn't make sense."

"You're only saying that because you see yourself as being the protector for these children," Claire answered easily. "But the truth is, Evan, there are three kids here. Three kids at once are difficult enough for the actual parents. It seems impossible for me to conceive that one man alone could raise them."

"I could do it," Evan insisted doggedly.

Claire chuckled lightly and shook her head. "I admire you for thinking you can. I admire you for *wanting* to do it, but I think you're wrong."

"And I think you're wrong."

Finally recognizing how serious he was, Claire also realized there was a purpose for this conversation and immediately understood what it was. "Your brothers agree with me, don't they?"

He sighed. "Yes."

"Well, take it as a good sign that each of them wants the responsibility for a child, and relax with the fact that you also get a child to raise."

"I don't want one. I want all three."

This time Claire sighed. "Evan, you can't have all three."

"Yeah, and you shouldn't even get a vote in this, but somehow you got one."

"I did?" Claire asked, pleased that the other Brewster men thought so highly of her. She knew she was becoming a friend to both of them, because Chas and Grant opened up to her much more than Evan. "That's very complimentary, but even without my vote, you're still outnumbered."

"True," Evan said, washing dishes with a vengeance Claire didn't quite understand. "But if you hadn't brought up the proposal in the first place, I wouldn't have to argue with my brothers now."

"Oh," Claire said miserably. Now she understood why he was behaving so oddly. The attraction wasn't the problem. He was mad at her. "I didn't mean to cause a rift between you."

"But you did."

"I didn't want to," Claire insisted. "I only wanted to help."

Evan unexpectedly spun on her. "Really? Why? Why would a twenty-three-year-old woman want to help three virtual strangers with their new kids?"

"Because I liked and respected your dad," Claire said quietly.

"Oh, baloney." Evan tossed his dishcloth into the empty sink. Without another word, he strode out of the room.

Not about to let that go without an explanation, Claire bounded after him. She caught his elbow and spun him around. "If you're accusing me of something, I have a right to know what it is."

"All right. You want to know what I think?" he demanded angrily. "I think you're keeping tabs on me."

"What?" Claire gasped.

"I think you're jealous that I'm dating Abby, so you're messing in my business and here every night..."

"You conceited lout!" she said, and pushed at him because he was so thickheaded. "I'm here because I'm helping your father the way he helped me. And *I'm* not the one staring at me day in and day out while he's supposed to be *dating* somebody else."

"I don't stare."

"Baloney," she said, using his word against him.

Having put the babies to bed, Chas and Grant were walking down the stairs. When they saw the scuffle taking place in the foyer, they jogged down the steps, grabbed keys from the curio cabinet and strode out the door.

"See you later," Chas called out in a singsong, then winked as he pulled the door closed behind him.

When they left, the house was eerily quiet. The kids were asleep, the chaperons were gone. Claire and Evan stood two feet apart, both angry, both breathing heavily from the strength of their convictions.

"Baloney," Claire repeated, this time with a little less force. "I see you staring at me all the time. You've almost kissed me twice."

"I never..."

"You have!" Claire insisted. "I don't mind that you don't *want* to be attracted to me, but at least have the decency to admit you are and stop trying to make me think I'm crazy...and quit dating Abby. Whether you know it or not, Evan, *that's* unfair."

She stopped herself and drew a long breath. Again the foyer resonated with silence.

"Look, I'm sorry. It's not my business if you're attracted to one person and dating another. If you can do that kind of thing, or if you have some other method of sorting out romantic attraction, I don't have a right to interfere. All I'm saying is Abby is my friend. If you're not really attracted to her, and you're using her for some reason or another, that's not fair."

With those words she left, apparently, Evan decided, forgetting that only he remained at the house with the babies.

He sat on the bottom step of the circular stairway, confused and alone. He knew Claire was right. What he was doing wasn't fair to Abby. Despite the fact that she had a child, she might not want to give up the opportunity to have more.

He sighed and dragged his hands down his face. Besides, Claire was right about something else. He really wasn't attracted to Abby. He was attracted to Claire and *that* was unfair to Abby.

The next day at lunchtime, Evan drove to the bed-and-breakfast. He privately told Abby he wouldn't be asking her out anymore and left feeling relieved.

Abby didn't seem to mind. She'd almost appeared relieved, too. That didn't bother Evan because it could be construed as an insult, but because he was beginning to wonder just how transparent he was around Claire.

If Abby suspected his feelings for Claire, and she'd seen them together only once, then it was just a matter of time before everyone at the mill knew.

After that everyone in town would know.

He *had* to get himself in line.

Chapter Five

After the fight between Evan and Claire, Grant insisted everyone spend time away from the babies. Claire had the night off and had just begun to clean her bathroom that evening when there was a knock at her door.

"Hi," Abby said when Claire answered.

"Hi," Abby's six-year-old son, Tyler, parroted. Though Tyler resembled his mother, he didn't have her coloring. Instead of the bountiful mane of flame-red curls, Tyler had straight black hair and serious brown eyes.

Claire stooped to greet him. "Hi, Tyler!" she said, then hugged him fiercely. "How are you?"

"I'm good. This is for you," he said, and handed an envelope made of brightly colored construction paper to her.

"This is for me?" Claire said, backing away from the door to offer him entry. "Why don't you come in while I read it?"

Claire led Abby and her son into the sunny yellow kitchen, and while she and Tyler took seats at the stools by the counter, Abby got everyone a glass of lemonade.

Knowing that Tyler had probably spent hours designing the envelope, Claire opened it with enthusiasm and fanfare. When she found the card and saw that "I love you" was scrawled across the front in huge childlike letters, tears filled her eyes and her lips trembled.

Because Claire had grown up not knowing her father, she understood completely that Tyler felt a void. But in Tyler's case the situation was worse. Both of his grandparents had died, and his only uncle had long ago moved from Brewster County in search of better things. For Tyler, there was only his mother, Abby, and Claire. He had an overflow of love to give and needed every bit as much in return.

"I love you, too," she whispered, and hugged him again before opening the card. "Let's see," she said, blinking back her tears. "It says here that you really liked my gift and you want to take me out to dinner for my birthday."

"To a real restaurant in Pittsburgh," Abby said from the refrigerator.

"You can't take me to Pittsburgh just for dinner."

Tyler turned his soulful brown eyes on her. "But Mom promised."

Abby shrugged. "See, I promised," she said, taking the stool beside Claire. "Unless you have plans with someone else?" she suggested coyly.

"You know I don't have plans with anyone else," Claire said.

"Maybe not now," Abby said slyly. "But I

wouldn't be so sure an invitation isn't just around the corner.''

Claire only looked at her. "What the heck are you talking about?''

"Tyler, why don't you go outside and see if Timmy Ringer is playing at the park across the street?''

Tyler immediately jumped off his stool. "Okay,'' he said, and was out of the kitchen within thirty seconds.

"You have to know what I'm talking about,'' Abby said when the front door closed on Tyler.

"I don't,'' Claire stated emphatically.

"I'm talking about Evan Brewster.''

Claire colored uncontrollably. "Evan Brewster?'' she asked, pretending innocence.

"Surely you realize he has feelings for you.''

Claire stared at Abby as if she'd grown a second head. "Abby, *you're* dating the man.''

"Not anymore,'' Abby said, then indifferently picked up her lemonade.

"Oh, Abby, if you broke up with him…''

"I didn't break up with him,'' Abby interrupted, smiling. "He came over today at lunch, said he hadn't meant to lead me on or give me the wrong impression, but things weren't working out like he thought they would.''

Claire swallowed. "Oh.''

"Oh, nothing,'' Abby said, lightly slapping Claire's arm as if to get her attention. "The first day the two of you came into the diner together, sparks virtually flew between you. When Evan asked me out and he talked mostly about how needed you were at the mill, I decided he was seeing me in a friendly way to ferret out information about you. So I've been giving it.''

"You went out with him to give him information about me?" Claire asked incredulously.

"I didn't realize we were dating," Abby said, setting her glass on the counter. "When we went out, it was more like two friends than two potential mates. I thought he was asking me out for companionship, not romance, and the way he behaved backed that up."

"Oh," Claire said, then immediately changed the subject. Like any true best friend, Abby let Claire switch topics, obviously sensing she either didn't want to talk about this or wasn't ready to talk about it.

Claire wasn't exactly sure which she was. She'd spent the past two weeks telling herself she was imagining that Evan was attracted to her, reminding herself she didn't want to be attracted to him, and trying to keep her thoughts and her hormones in neutral around him. Abby's information not only confused her, it left her numb. Because Evan kept backing away, Claire never considered how she'd actually feel if he asked her out...or touched her...or kissed her. The mere thought gave her goose bumps.

When the elevator doors opened the next morning, Claire looked up to see that Evan had arrived for work. What she was thinking or feeling must have been written all over her face, because when their eyes met, both of them seemed to freeze. Claire couldn't even squeeze "good morning" past her lips.

She thought Evan might be equally speechless, but he walked toward his office door, breaking the spell. "Give me a minute to get settled," he said, "then bring in the mail."

When he was gone, Claire collapsed against her

desk. She had to stop imagining things that weren't there.

She knew why she was doing it. In spite of the way Evan had avoided admitting or denying an attraction during their argument, Abby had more or less led Claire's thoughts back in that direction when she told Claire Evan had talked about her on their dates. In her overactive imagination, Claire had blown that piece of news way out of proportion. The truth undoubtedly was that Abby and Evan didn't have enough in common to hold a complete conversation and Evan had probably grabbed on to the one mutual friend they had...her.

And that was that. He hadn't talked about her because he was interested in her, only because she was a convenient topic with Abby.

Gathering her spiral notebook and all the other assorted files, papers and projects she needed to discuss with Evan, Claire brought herself in line with that logic. But when she turned from the filing cabinet to enter his office and found him staring at her, her knees became rubbery and weak.

Still, he looked away so fast and behaved so neutrally when she entered his office that she once again questioned her sanity.

"Potter file," she said, handing the brown folder across the desk to Evan along with a piece of mail. "This is a contract that needs to be renegotiated."

He nodded.

"Bingham file with phone message you received when you were out yesterday afternoon."

As the words came out of Claire's mouth, she realized he had been breaking off his relationship with Abby yesterday afternoon, and it felt as if all the air evaporated from the room. Her gaze jumped to Evan, who again hadn't reacted at all. Claire nearly closed her eyes in despair. Would she ever be able to control herself around him? Was she so desperate to have him want her that she was going to exaggerate everything he did?

No. Absolutely not, she decided, and rose from her seat when they were through with their business. She knew that if she didn't soon get a hold of herself, she would embarrass herself mightily, and Evan, too, and that would be the end of the job she couldn't do without. She had no choice but to support herself. She didn't have an inheritance or a family to fall back on.

She was on her own in a small town where opportunities didn't often come along. She wasn't going to destroy this one because she couldn't get her hormones under control.

"Bottles?"

"Bottles."

"Babies?"

"Babies."

"Okay, looks like we're set, then," Evan said, and began climbing the steps to the nursery. He held two children and one bottle and Claire carried one child and two bottles. Everything was back to normal.

After getting settled in two of the rockers, both Claire and Evan took bottles from the bottle holder hooked to the arm of her chair.

"It amazes me that you can do that," she announced suddenly in the silence of the nursery.

"What?" he asked. The room was nearly black. The only light came from a small ceramic rainbow lamp on a table behind them. All three babies sucked noisily.

"Feed two kids at once," Claire answered quietly.

"They're feeding themselves. I'm just holding them so they can do it."

"Yeah, you're right," she said, her attention caught by the two adorable little girls he held. She no longer had to be reminded that Taylor was the one with black hair and Annie had the slightly curly sandy-brown hair. Not only were they physically different, but Taylor and Annie also had distinct personalities. Taylor was sweet and quiet and loved to cuddle, whereas Annie was curious and noisy and loved to gnaw. Fingers and noses were turning into her favorite teething tools.

Claire and Evan fed the children in silence after that, putting them in their beds when they were certain the babies were sound asleep. They left the nursery without a word and made their way down the circular stairway.

"Would you like popcorn with TV tonight?" Claire asked when they reached the foyer.

"Actually, I was going to tell you that you could have the night off."

"But you're here alone with the kids!" Claire protested. "I know it seems okay when they're sleeping, but what if all three wake up before Chas and Grant get home?"

Smirking confidently, Evan said, "I've done it before."

Reminded that she'd recently walked out on him, Claire winced. "But you shouldn't have had to."

"No, but you were right about Abby," Evan said, leading Claire to the kitchen, where he extracted microwave popcorn from one of the cupboards. "I told her as much the next day."

Claire took a seat on a stool. "I know, she told me."

"Okay, then," Evan said, focusing on the popcorn in the microwave as if he needed to pay attention to it or it wouldn't get cooked. "That's the end of that."

"Right," Claire said, feeling incredibly uncomfortable. The air was always charged with something when they were together, but tonight it seemed supercharged. She wished she'd had more experience with men so she could understand what was going on between them.

For the next two minutes, only the hum of the microwave filled the air, then, mercifully, the buzzer sounded. Evan pulled out the popcorn with a sigh of relief and grabbed a bowl. "Let's hit the TV."

Because he virtually ran out of the room, Claire took a minute to compose herself. When she finally reached the family room, Evan had poured the popcorn into the bowl and set it on a low table in front of a chair at least six feet away from the couch. To add insult to injury, he was sitting at the opposite end of the couch.

She bit her bottom lip. Boy, she and Abby had certainly missed the mark on this one. Evan was not interested in Claire, either, and he was taking great pains to make sure she got the message.

As if realizing the adults were having a difficult time on their own, one of the babies began to cry.

Relieved, Evan bounced from the sofa. "Got it!" he said, and scrambled from the room. But before he'd even disappeared from view, another baby began to cry, and Claire scrambled after him.

When she entered the nursery, Evan was seated on a rocker patting Annie's back, so Claire walked over, pulled Cody from the crib and took him to a rocker. Neither one of them said a word. They weren't supposed to. As long as there was no disruption, the children would probably fall back to sleep. In five minutes, Annie did, and Evan tiptoed out of the room. A minute later, Cody followed suit and Claire slipped from the nursery and returned to the family room.

But to her surprise, Evan wasn't there. Instead, she found him in the den. He glanced up when she entered. "Something I can do for you?"

"No, I was just wondering what you wanted to watch tonight."

"Nothing," Evan answered absently, then rose from the high backed chair behind the mahogany desk to rifle through his briefcase for a file. "You watch what you want and leave when you want. I'm fine."

"Did I do something?" Claire asked, confused because they'd resolved their argument so he couldn't be angry with her anymore.

"No," Evan answered, still standing by the leather sofa, rummaging through his briefcase.

"Okay, then maybe I can help you," Claire said, bounding over to the sofa and flipping through the file he had discarded. But their hands accidentally brushed and Evan sprang back as if he'd been burned.

Exasperated, Claire only stared at him. "Why do you keep running from me?"

Frustrated, frazzled, he turned away from her. "I'm not running from you."

She grabbed his arm and insisted he face her. "Yes, you are."

He squeezed his eyes shut. "Why don't you just go home?"

"Why don't you tell me what's wrong?"

"You want to know what's wrong?" he demanded softly. "The situation keeps getting worse and worse, harder and harder to deal with. Every time I'm around you, I want to do this…"

He suddenly cupped her face in his hands and lifted it ever so gently until his lips touched hers. He didn't close his eyes, and for several seconds, neither did she, but the feeling of his mouth on hers was too delicious, too wonderful to endure, and her eyelids drifted shut. When they did, he pressed his mouth against hers with a little more pressure. When she didn't protest that, he deepened the kiss, and of their own volition her arms looped around his neck. While his hands found the small of her back and urged her forward, he used his tongue to part her lips, then slowly slid it inside her mouth.

Every muscle in her body went limp, even as her heart rate seemed to triple. Kissing Evan was so sensual she could have easily tumbled in head first and let every luscious sensation take her, but her foggy brain reminded her that he'd more or less kissed her to prove a point. He didn't want to do this. He might not be able to stop himself, but he didn't want to do this.

Pride straightened her spine and caused her to pull away.

"I'm sorry," she whispered and stepped back several feet.

"I'll bet you are," he said hoarsely, shifting farther away from her.

"Not for the reasons you think," Claire said, then

swallowed hard. "I'm not sorry you kissed me, I'm sorry I pushed you into it."

"You didn't push me," Evan began, but he paused and rubbed his hand across the back of his neck because they both knew that she had—if only because she wouldn't give him the space he needed to deal with this attraction in his own way.

For an agonizing minute Claire wished for a miracle, she wished the phone would ring, one of the kids would cry or something. But when nothing happened to break the awful silence, she knew the only way out of this was going to be with the truth. The whole truth. No matter how embarrassing.

"I'd have to be blind not to see that you might be attracted to me but you don't want to be."

Apparently opting for not speaking as a defense of sorts, he drew a breath and nodded.

Claire swallowed. "So, I might as well come right out and admit that I have my reasons for not wanting to be attracted to you, either."

His head came up so quickly and his face registered such relief that Claire almost laughed. "The truth is," she said, then paused to gather her courage. "I was illegitimate. That's why I'm so much older than my brothers and sisters. That's why I know how to care for babies. I was a teenager by the time most of them were born. In a lot of ways, I feel like an interloper in my own family."

The revelation explained many things to Evan. It didn't make him feel any less desperately foolish for wanting something he couldn't have. Nor did it make him any less aroused from having kissed her. If she'd tasted any better, if she'd felt any better pressed against him, he would have died from the sheer pleasure of it. He'd never before had this oh-my-God-she's-so-good shock when he'd kissed a woman. His stomach fell to the floor, the blood still roared in his ears. It took every ounce of strength he possessed not to haul her back into his arms when she pulled away from him.

Still, her explanation didn't cover why she didn't want to have anything to do with him—and almost made him feel she was accusing him of being a snob.

Forced into conversation, he cleared his throat, hoping that when he tried to speak actual words would come out. "What does that have to do with anything?"

"My father was rich and important and my mother didn't fit into his world."

"Oh," he said, then almost laughed hysterically. If Claire was trying to tell him she didn't fit into his world, all she had to do was look around. She not only was in his world, she sometimes ruled his world. Still, he didn't argue.

"I spent the first ten years of my life in abject poverty because my mother's parents kicked her out when she got pregnant. I vowed I would never go through that again, and vowed I wouldn't make the same mistake my mother had."

His forehead furrowed. "Are you talking about dating people in a different social sphere, or are you talking about having sex?" he asked curiously, unable to resist. Not merely because he was hungry for any piece of personal information, but because it seemed she was leading him to a conclusion that almost floored him. For all her business savvy, for all her sass and confidence, his Claire was a virgin.

A virgin?

For a minute it looked like she wouldn't answer him, but she smiled suddenly and said, "Actually, I guess it could be either."

He stared at her. "You're kidding, right?"

She shook her head. "Nope. Evan, you don't go to bed hungry at night without learning a lesson or two. I might have been young, but I understand what had happened." She paused to shrug. "I don't even know my dad because my mother didn't want him in our lives, reminding her of the past. I lost my dad and grew up in poverty because two people made a mistake."

Flabbergasted, Evan stared at her.

"So," she said, nervously backing toward the door. "That more or less settles that. I don't want to be attracted to you. You don't want to be attracted to me. Both of our curiosities have been satisfied with one little kiss and one short conversation. So what do you say we just call ourselves even, act like mature adults, and get on with the rest of our lives?"

Smiling stiffly, Evan nodded his agreement and even gave her a funny little wave good-bye to show there were no hard feelings, and he could act like an adult about this if she could. But the truth was he was having trouble assimilating that someone as beautiful, thoughtful, sweet and adorable as Claire could have avoided having a man make love to her for twenty-three years.

The worst part about it was everything she told him about herself might give him more reason to stay away from her, but those same things also seemed to make her more right for him, more like the woman he was looking for. A struggle between integrity and

wanting was constantly being waged in his head. And
with this new information the wanting was winning.

Still, he more than saw her point about behaving
like mature adults. He had bigger, better reasons to
stay away from her than she imagined, so he had no
choice but to behave.

But if he had a choice, she would be his before the
year was out!

Chapter Six

"Do you have your tickets?" Claire asked Chas as she nervously straightened his tie.

Patting the breast pocket of his jacket, Chas nodded. "Right here."

"Okay, then how about a clean shirt?"

"I packed two just in case."

"And you have extra money?"

Exasperated, Evan pushed away from the door-jamb. "Claire, he's thirty. If he isn't smart enough to take extra money, then he should be smart enough to have his bank card."

"I guess," Claire agreed, then gnawed her bottom lip. "It's just that this is the first time he's been away from home."

"He lived away from home for two years," Grant put in, his mouth twisting awkwardly as if he was trying to keep from laughing.

"This is his first interview," Claire argued, sweetly annoyed. "I'm nervous for him."

"Don't be," Evan said. He put his arm around Claire's shoulders and turned her in the direction of the family room. "He can take care of himself."

"I suppose," Claire agreed quietly.

"I know," Evan said emphatically, giving her a little push. "Go watch TV. Grant and I will be in in a minute."

The second she was gone, Grant said, "Get where you need to go, don't get involved with any women...at least until after you've had your interview, and get home quickly because you're going to owe me and Evan big time for covering for you for three days."

Chas sighed dramatically. "I liked Claire's sermon better than yours. Bring her back. Let her say goodbye."

"Not on your life," Evan said, shoving Chas out the door. "Just remember, Grant and I know you better than Claire does, and if you don't do what you're supposed to do, we'll tell her all your secrets."

Chas glared at his brothers. "The whole purpose for leaving town to make your mistakes is so you don't have to live them down."

"Then you shouldn't call your older brothers to bail you out of jail," Grant said, smirking.

"Whatever." Chas bounded down the front porch steps. When he reached the bottom, he turned and grinned. "Have fun with the babies for the next three days."

"Oh, we will," Evan said, then closed the door. "What do you think his chances are for survival without us?"

"As long as he doesn't meet a woman, he ought to do just fine," Grant replied, slapping Evan on the back. "And speaking of women, you're going to be by yourself with Claire for the next two days because I've got to be in Savannah for meetings day after tomorrow. Think you can handle it?"

"Claire and I have handled the babies by ourselves before. We won't—"

Grant stopped him with a hard look. "You know what I'm talking about."

Evan took a deep breath, considered lying and opted for the truth only because it was less complicated. "Claire and I talked about this. We decided we might be attracted to each other, but it's not right, so we're acting like mature adults."

"Boy, are you stupid," Grant said, then turned to jog up the staircase. "I'm going to pack, then I'm going out for an hour or two. You and Claire can start acting like adults one day early."

Evan shook his head in wonder at the things his older brother considered humorous, and walked into the family room. "Want popcorn?"

"Nah," Claire replied absently. "I'm getting sick of it."

"Chips? Cheese curls? Crackers?"

She shook her head. "No."

"Can I turn off the TV?"

That caught her attention and she gave him a puzzled frown. "Why?"

"Well, Grant just told me he's leaving for Savannah tomorrow. He has meetings."

Claire shrugged. "So? We've handled the kids by ourselves before."

"Exactly what I told him." Evan smiled, covering something that felt oddly like disappointment. Over the past week, she'd been so relaxed around him he felt old and foolish, as if he'd imagined she was attracted to him. Of course, her being comfortable was a good thing because he needed her, so he was glad everything had worked out the way it had. He just never realized how much the emotion "glad" felt like a slow, dull ache.

The next day, Grant brought the triplets to work. "We seem to have made one miscalculation in our plans," he said, steering the three-seated stroller into Claire's office.

She dropped her pen, realizing they'd forgotten they would need someone to care for the kids during the day. "What time does your plane leave?"

"It's already gone," Grant said casually, as if he accepted life's little confusions now that he was partially responsible for three kids. "But I can drive down and still check into a hotel in time to catch a few hours' sleep before the meeting tomorrow morning."

By this time Evan had walked out to Claire's office to see what the commotion was about. "Oh, boy," he said when he saw the kids. Taylor gave him a toothless grin. Annie put a teething ring in her mouth. Cody tried to worm out of his seat. "Looks like we forgot something."

"I think we're all still operating in single time," Grant said, his black suit rumpled, his hair disheveled, his tie partially undone. "I'm going to have to drive, so I have to leave now or I won't get any sleep before the meeting."

"Do whatever you have to do," Evan said simply. "Claire and I will take care of this."

"I have an idea," Claire said suddenly. "My sister Kelly could use some extra money, so why don't we call her and see if she can rustle up a friend or two to help her look after the kids over the next few days.''

"Kelly has experience with babies?" Evan asked cautiously.

"She's the oldest of six children, remember?"

"That's perfect," Grant said, snapping his fingers. "Looks like we've got ourselves a daytime sitter."

"For a while," Claire cautioned. "You don't want to leave three kids with a bunch of teenagers indefinitely."

"No," Evan agreed, reaching down to free a squirming Cody from his seat. "But they'll do in a pinch. Call her," he instructed, and Claire nodded.

"Great," Grant said, stepping into the elevator again. "I'll see you guys in a few days." The elevator door began to close, but he caught it, grinning smugly. "If you have any problems, don't call me. I'll be getting eight uninterrupted hours of sleep."

With that the elevator doors swished closed and Claire gasped, "Oh my gosh, Evan. You're going to be by yourself with three kids tonight!"

"Are you sure you're okay with this?" Evan asked, billowing the fitted sheet in the air as he helped Claire make up what she figured had to be the sixth bedroom in the house. She supposed that was fairly normal in a mansion, but she also knew her mother's family would feel as if they'd died and gone to heaven if they ever saw this place.

"I'm fine," she said, catching the sheet as it fell so she could pull her side around its corners.

"Claire, this isn't as simple as it sounds. You're

staying overnight, unchaperoned, with one of the Brewsters. Tomorrow your name could be mud.''

"Tomorrow your name could be mud,'' Claire countered, a little annoyed by the stereotype. "You're staying overnight with a woman who's ten years younger than you are.''

Evan laughed. "Claire, in 'man world' that would enhance my reputation.''

"Yeah, right, whatever,'' she said, pretending to ignore him. But in truth, she had considered this carefully. Not because of her reputation. That hadn't really crossed her mind. What had crossed her mind over and over again was the way her attraction to him had grown stronger, more powerful...more sensual, since he'd kissed her. She remembered the taste of his mouth. She remembered the softness of his lips. She could recall everything so vividly, just the thought made her shiver.

"Claire?''

"Huh?'' Abruptly brought out of her reverie, Claire blinked at him.

"I said, do you think you'll need another blanket?''

She swallowed. "No. I'll be fine.''

"You're sure?'' he asked seriously.

Claire forced a smile. "I'm fine,'' she said, realizing she was far, far from it, but determined not to let him know that, since he didn't seem to be having any trouble at all with the attraction anymore. Whatever his reason for wanting to stay away from her, she recognized it was a good one because it was big enough or important enough that he seemed to have lost any feeling he might have had for her.

Cody awakened at two-thirty, and Evan didn't even think. He rolled out of bed, took a bottle from the small refrigerator they'd put in the nursery, and set it in a warmer before he reached down and checked to see if Cody needed to be changed. The noise woke Annie, and she groaned a little, then began to cry in earnest. Forgetting everything but the concentration he needed to stay awake while he changed the baby and got him fed, Evan didn't have the presence of mind to realize that when Claire came in to get Annie, she'd be wearing nightclothes.

When she pushed open the door and stumbled into the room half-asleep, her hair wild and sexily tousled, her sheer floral robe billowing around her and her pink satin pajamas clinging to her sleep-warmed body, he looked away and squeezed his eyes shut, wondering what the hell he could have done in a past life that would sentence him to this torment.

Since she didn't seem affected by the sight of him in loose-fitting sweats and shirtless, Evan's ego deflated somewhat. Without a word, he took his seat on the rocker with Cody and snuggled the baby against his chest as he fed him.

Having changed Annie, Claire joined him on her own rocker. After about two minutes, she whispered, "Why didn't Taylor get up?"

Evan shrugged. If she could be nonchalant, so could he. "I don't have a clue. Sometimes I think they can sense when there are only two of us available. She'll probably start to cry the minute I put Cody in his crib."

"If she does, I'll get her," Claire volunteered generously.

Evan smiled tiredly. "I'll get her."

Claire nodded her agreement and the conversation

ended. As if on cue, Taylor began to cry once Evan
was free. He prepared a bottle, checked her for wet-
ness, then took her to a rocker. When Annie finished
her bottle, Claire rocked her back to sleep, put her in
her crib and left without a word.

Evan leaned back in his rocker and closed his eyes.
What a world. He was alone in a house with a beautiful woman, and instead of even attempting to make
long, lingering love to her, instead of trying to seduce
her into a relationship, he was rocking a baby.

Evan's forehead puckered as he contemplated the
thought. In the first place, he knew why he couldn't
seduce Claire into a relationship and he couldn't believe he'd forgotten. But the more overpowering,
more confusing realization was that this was the first
time he'd wanted to make love with a woman purely
for the pleasure of making love—without regret, re-
morse or thoughts of procreation—in nearly eight
years. It puzzled him so much he forgot all about Taylor, who lost her bottle and screamed at the top of her
lungs.

Evan guided the nipple back to her mouth, then
whispered, "If you think you want to scream, you
should be me."

Claire let Evan sleep in the next morning, and when
he finally awakened, he bounced up in bed as if someone had poured water on his head. Wiser in the day-
light hours, he grabbed a robe and ran into the nursery. None of the babies was there and the house was
silent.

Confused and more than a little worried, he flew
down the steps, checked the empty kitchen, looked in
the empty family room and almost fell to his knees

with relief when he found Claire and all three babies in the den.

"What are you doing?" he asked with deadly quiet.

"Reviewing the Monroe contract to make sure they didn't take out anything."

Evan took two slow, deliberate steps into the den. Annie let out a yelp for attention. Cody said something that sounded very much like "Hey." Taylor slapped a ball. "How did you do this?"

She didn't look up from the contract. "I made a deal with them."

"They can't even talk, Claire. A deal is completely out of the question."

"I make a lot of eye contact."

With everybody but him, Evan thought sourly as he sank to the sofa. "What are you looking at?" he groused at Cody, who laughed heartily. "Yeah, that's right, kid. There are just some things women do better than men."

"My competence has nothing to do with being a woman," Claire said, again without looking up. "It's experience, nothing more." This time she graced him with a smile. A lovely, golden morning smile. He noticed that though she'd dressed the kids, she still wore her pajamas and robe, and a steaming cup of coffee and plate of toast sat on the desk. That could only mean she wasn't quite as efficient as she looked.

Only about twice as efficient as he and his brothers were.

"I'm going upstairs to get dressed," he said, rising from the sofa.

She smiled again. "Okay. I'll go up when you're done."

He sat again. "You go first." It was bad enough

thinking of her showering upstairs; thinking about her down here in pajamas while he showered would be his undoing. This way when he showered she would be dressed. It was frivolous, but he wasn't questioning why he thought the things he did anymore.

She gave him a puzzled look, but rose. "Sure. No problem."

He smiled.

She smiled.

"Would you go already?" he asked when it seemed as if she planned on standing in front of him in her pajamas all day.

She left him, floral robe floating around her, and Taylor squealed playfully. "Either you've got an awfully good memory or you can read minds," he said, and almost took her from the playpen, but he stopped himself. Maybe the reason Claire had better luck with the kids was that she didn't always spoil them. Maybe if he watched her performance with the babies more than he watched her behind when she bent over to pick up a toy, or her breasts when she nestled one of the triplets, or her lips when she brushed a kiss across somebody's head, he'd learn something.

"Bottles are in the fridge. Diapers are in the nursery. Instructions for lunch are on the counter."

"Go!" Claire's younger sister Kelly said with a laugh, and nearly pushed her out the door. Where Claire had dark hair and pale blue eyes, Kelly had blond hair and dark brown eyes. Claire was tall and well built. Kelly was short and thin.

The two helpers she brought with her were almost her clones. Standing in the foyer, smiling at Evan as if he were the captain of the football team, both grinned at him. Evan caught Claire's elbow. "Yes, let's go."

"You seem to have a certain appeal to younger women," she said with a laugh walking with him to his sport utility vehicle.

"Really?" he said through gritted teeth, then slammed the door on her.

"Now, don't get mad," she said, as he took the seat behind the steering wheel.

"I'm not mad," he insisted, but he was. For someone who was supposed to appeal to younger women, he didn't seem to have any effect on her. Lately, she was completely oblivious to him. Evan knew that was good. He knew they weren't supposed to have a relationship because they weren't right for each other. But, damn it, if he couldn't ooom to shake the attraction, it didn't seem fair that she could.

"Touchy this morning," she mumbled, then wisely occupied herself with a file.

"You don't know the half of it," he replied out loud, but inwardly he began to lecture himself. He knew the rules. He knew the unofficial pact they'd made. But more than that, any woman who was as good with kids as Claire was deserved to have as many as she wanted. That was the bottom line. He couldn't give her what she needed. *Couldn't.* It was a physical impossibility. Not his fault. Not hers. Nature's.

He drew a long, resigned breath. There. He felt better. Then he scowled. No, he didn't.

Damn it. He wanted life to be fair. If he couldn't have her, at least she should suffer as much as he was suffering.

He deflated again. That wasn't fair.

But who was he to talk about fair? Since he'd never felt this kind of unreasonable attraction before, he didn't know how to handle it. He almost believed it such an anomaly that it would burn out the first time they had sex....

Which they would never have because she was determined to stay a virgin.

He couldn't win.

She was officially going to drive him crazy.

Gentlemen, place your bets on location and time. The lady seems to have the advantage.

Chapter Seven

Claire couldn't understand why he was acting so oddly. At first she thought it was because he couldn't handle the triplets without his brothers, but she knew that wasn't true. He loved them enough that taking care of them came naturally.

And she loved seeing him with the babies. It was fun to watch Chas and Grant with the triplets, but Evan was something spectacular. Especially with Cody. Taylor and Annie loved Evan, but they were enamored with Grant and Chas. Cody was Evan's little man. Every time Evan entered the room, Cody watched him with big, anxious blue eyes, waiting for him to reach into the playpen or crib and pull him into his arms. Even if he was sitting with another of his brothers, Cody would squeal until Evan took him. So Cody was perfectly content, but with Chas and Grant out of town, the girls had become slightly fussy and unpredictable, almost as bad as Evan. Claire definitely had her hands full.

"Have we had *any* luck with that ad yet?" Evan demanded marching into her office after the mail had come and been sorted.

Claire took a long breath. "No, Evan, nannies aren't exactly plentiful here on the mountain."

"Do you mean to tell me there isn't even a lonely grandmother who'd like to watch some kids?"

"Lonely grandmothers recognize they can't handle three babies alone."

"An out-of-work mom?"

"Is probably watching her own kids."

"An out-of-work anybody?"

"Brewster Lumber employs just about everybody in this county," Claire reminded him calmly. "The people you don't employ work in the city because they *want* to work in the city." She paused and sighed. "Brewster County is more trees than people, Evan. We're going to have trouble finding someone."

"What about day care?"

"Twenty miles away. We're not as progressive as a metropolitan area," she said firmly, because he didn't seem to be getting the picture. "You're just going to have to work around some of these inconveniences."

He tossed his hands in the air and stormed back into his office. "It's no wonder my brothers and I left this place two years ago."

Claire would have liked to make a snappy comeback to that. Specifically she would remind him that he'd not only returned, he'd told her he believed this small, sparsely populated rural area was the best place to raise children. However, she thought better of it. In spite of everything, Claire had believed they would remain friends. But after the way he'd been behaving the past two days, she knew that wasn't going to happen. And it hurt her. Disappointed her. She missed the possibility that she could be romantically involved with someone as sexy, sophisticated and wonderful as Evan, but losing his friendship was even worse.

Seeing him pour himself into work, Claire frowned. She didn't believe they had to give up their friendship because they couldn't be romantic. In fact, she intended to prove it to him—even if he bit her head off on her first few tries.

Claire watched Evan hang up his phone and run both hands down his face. Because she knew the call had been from Chas, she walked into his office the minute he cradled the receiver.

"What's up?" she asked cautiously

"You remember that I told you Grant couldn't come home because his business partner was having some trouble and couldn't even come in to work, let alone handle their construction company himself?"

Fearing the worst, Claire nodded. "Yes."

"Well, now Chas isn't returning until Tuesday or Wednesday. The partner who interviewed him for the law firm wants him to meet the other partners. He'll meet two on Monday and two on Tuesday. He hopes to come home that night, but he might be held up until Wednesday."

Claire took a short breath for courage and said, "That isn't necessarily bad. Having the kids all weekend without help isn't unusual. Real parents don't get any time off, you know."

He scowled at her, obviously realizing that if he argued, he proved her point about dividing up the triplets and giving one to each brother to raise.

"I'm fine with this," he said, but Claire knew he wasn't.

She suspected that was because they were stuck spending more time together, and she decided this would be the perfect weekend to prove to him that just because they couldn't be lovers, it didn't mean they couldn't be friends. If it killed her, she was going to be nice to him all weekend and incredibly accommodating to show that they could get beyond this.

When she was gone, Evan squeezed his eyes shut. There was a limit as to how many showers a man could take and probably a limit to how much cold water a man could tolerate before his heart gave way from the shock.

That evening when Claire returned from driving her sister and her friends to their homes, she entered the house carrying a huge duffel bag.

"What's this?" Evan asked curiously.

"Overnight clothes."

"Are you wearing seven pairs of pajamas tonight or several shirts tomorrow?"

"Neither," Claire answered cheerfully. "I just decided there was no reason for me to travel to and from my home to get clothes every day. In this bag, I have clothes for the weekend and clothes for Monday. You won't be without me for one minute."

Evan forced a smile. "Great," he said, and turned to walk into the kitchen. Her jaunts home or to the grocery store were his salvation. They were the minutes he took to cool off and calm down. Now they were gone. Like he said, "Great."

"So what are we making for supper?" she asked, following him into the kitchen. Tonight she wore sunny-yellow shorts, a neat white blouse and sandals that showed off perfect feet with painted toenails. They reminded him that she was different—as in female—and his toes curled. Lately, it didn't take too much to remind him that they were male and female. He was sex starved, and she looked like the appetizer, main course and dessert all rolled into one.

Inspiration struck and he spun to face her. "How about if I surprise you with dinner?"

"You?" she asked incredulously. "You can't cook your way out of a paper bag."

Not willing to spend another forty minutes bumping into each other, wishing for something he couldn't have, Evan said, "Then why don't you surprise me?"

She thought about that. "Okay," she reluctantly agreed.

"Good, I'll go check on the kids," Evan said, feeling that he'd finally won a round. It wasn't fair. It really wasn't fair that fate dangled her in front of his face, tempting him with something he couldn't have, and now it seemed fate was laughing at him, taunting him, tormenting him because she didn't understand. She was perfectly fine with them being friends. Her libido wasn't suffering. His ego was, but her libido wasn't. In fact, if he didn't know better, he'd think she'd be perfectly happy with nothing more than friendship, while he suffered in silence.

He sighed. The bottom line was if he didn't let himself be tormented, then he wouldn't be tormented. He would simply stay the hell away from her.

She found him in the den fifteen minutes later and he only stared at her. He thought for sure cooking dinner would keep her out of his line of vision for at least forty minutes. Instead she stood before him, her long, satiny legs exposed below her shorts, her big blue eyes bright and cheerful.

"We're not having hot dogs again, are we?" he asked in dismay.

From the way he was constantly drawn to her beautiful eyes, where most of her emotion shone through like a beacon, he concluded it was her personality that appealed to him more than her legs. Though if there had been some sort of question about whether or not to be attracted to her, her body would have definitely given her the advantage over other women. But she didn't need an advantage. She was sweet, sharp and sexy. What a combination. It was no wonder he was floundering. He was virtually living with an intelligent woman who had the disposition of a saint and the legs of a goddess.

"No, I popped in a casserole."

And she could cook.

"Good Lord," he said, his mouth watering as the aroma wafted through the air. He was *damned*. He didn't just like this woman, he adored her. Spending more time with her or challenging himself to find a weak spot only proved her more perfect for him.

"Anyway, what do you think about taking the kids to work with us Monday morning?"

"Your sister can't baby-sit?" he asked, his mind shifting away from her lips, her sparkling blue eyes, her long legs and her absolute perfection in the kitchen.

"She could, but she and her friends aren't going to be able to cover for us all the time, and I don't want to use up our favors."

He saw her point. "Okay, we'll just have to pack everything up and—"

"Why don't we buy a second set of everything for the office and set up a nursery play area in the office so that we don't have to move back and forth?"

"Okay," he agreed, concluding she was a genius. A wonderful, perfect, sexy genius who could always think even when his brain was clouded. God, he needed her....

Even as he thought the last, his mind suddenly cleared. *He needed her.* Maybe fate wasn't tormenting him as much as it was trying to tell him something. She wasn't like every other woman he'd ever met. She didn't merely appeal to him physically. She didn't merely complement his personality. They didn't merely work well together, interact well together and love the kids equally as much. Everything they did and thought meshed. Maybe there was something about her that offset the fact that he couldn't have kids? Maybe they really were made for each other?

He stopped that thought right where it was because this wasn't something a person decided in two minutes. He would consider this, ponder it, dwell on it, determine ramifications, then think about it some more, because if she really was perfect for him, if he wasn't actually envisioning things that weren't there because his hormones were officially controlling his brain, then he had to bare his soul before he made any moves. If he didn't, he wouldn't be fair. And he had to be fair. She deserved fair, but more than that, if he let himself fall, if he dared to let himself believe there might be a future for them, it would be a pain worse than death if she rejected him.

He didn't say anything that night, but having that slim hope in the back of his mind relaxed him and life went back to normal again. He didn't monitor his staring. He didn't try to control what he said. He relaxed. And so did she. So much so that he didn't stop her when she plopped down beside him on the sofa Saturday night. Sharing the same bowl of popcorn, they inched closer and closer under the pretense of having easier access to their snack. But in the end, when their shoulders were brushing and their thighs kept touching, Evan began to see that something like gravity had them in its grip.

He waited for her to shift over.

She didn't move.

She waited for him to jerk away.

He didn't.

An odd tingling sensation enveloped Claire. The sense of rightness was back, but this time it was peppered with awareness she didn't have before he kissed her. A smart woman would be moving away right now. She knew that because she knew he had a reason for not wanting to be attracted to her, but she also knew that she was hungry. She'd spent her whole life looking for someone—anyone who understood her and cared about her—and now not only had she found him, but he was as attracted to her physically as she was attracted to him. It seemed *wrong* to walk away from this without even a tiny taste of what could be between them.

"Claire, one of us is going to have to shift a little bit."

She swallowed. "So, why don't you?"

"I figured you'd have sense enough to do that."

"No," she said, and shook her head. "No sense here."

"Come on, Claire, dealing with this is hard enough for me. You've got to keep your wits about you."

She shook her head again. "I don't think so. If you really and truly don't want me, then you should be man enough to handle this."

"It isn't that I don't want you…"

She stopped him with one finger over his lips. "Then kiss me, for pete's sake."

If her eyes hadn't been so blue and her simple, uncomplicated feelings for him so readily evident in their warm depths, he probably could have resisted. But he could see her emotion. He could see everything he'd been searching for during the past several years. He could see things he thought he couldn't have. He could see things he knew he didn't deserve. And he was tired. Tired of fighting, tired of wanting, tired of being right beside her every day, all day long, and unable to touch what kept brushing his fingertips.

He lowered his head, feathering his lips across hers softly because fear enveloped him. If he pushed too hard, she would run. If he wanted too much, too soon, she would disappear.

Watching her eyes, watching the acceptance, he let his eyelids drift closed and deepened the kiss, his tongue playing with the corners of her mouth before separating her lips and delving inside.

For Claire it was overwhelming. Her heart had long ago figured out that she loved this man. Her brain had come to accept it when she refused to let him ignore her. Now her body was coming under an attack she didn't quite understand. The intimacy of kissing him was so intense it was almost painful. Not because of the physical closeness, but because of their emotional closeness. Their shared life added a dimension to the experience that left her breathless. He knew her. He didn't have all the exact details, but he knew her likes and dislikes, her strengths and weaknesses. In the same way, she felt she knew him inside and out, and in a sense she did. As his tongue stroked across hers, it wasn't the intrusion of a stranger, but the welcome arrival of a trusted friend. The introduction of romantic love seemed like a logical next step to everything else they were building together.

Frightened by lack of experience, but buoyed by the notion that this stimulating, exciting, mind-numbing next step was right, she looped her arms around his neck, pressing herself against him, and basked in his groan of pleasure.

As she sensed her power, her boldness grew. When he kissed her, she kissed him back, mimicking the movements of his tongue, dancing with him, teasing him, toying with him. He rubbed his hands down her back. She rubbed her hands down his back. For her it was something like a sensual game of follow the leader, but the satisfaction came from both sides. Touching him, discovering him fulfilled long-held desires, but being touched filled her with shivers of anticipation.

The give-and-take was easy and good until what started off slow and deliberate became hurried and desperate. Somehow she slid down on the couch. Somehow their arms and legs became tangled. Somehow the kisses that were so delicious and satisfying became frustrating.

She didn't protest when the thrusts of his tongue grew deeper and harder. She met him thrust for thrust as hungry as he was for something she didn't quite understand. When he began unbuttoning her blouse, her hands moved to the fasteners on his shirt. When he pushed her blouse out of the way, she shifted to accommodate him. When she began inching his shirt up his back, he growled and yanked it off.

In what seemed like seconds, they were lying together on the sofa and kissing as if there would never be another chance.

For Evan the experience was hot, immediate and insufferably intoxicating. He felt her trembling with need, and he mirrored it in his own trembling need.

Reveling in the warmth of her skin against his, the hard pebbles of her nipples pressing into his chest, he felt himself grow harder still, until he thought he'd burst if he couldn't have her right then, right there on the sofa.

But he remembered she was a virgin and knew he had to be careful and gentle. He slowed the kiss, drawing them back from mindless passion to a more coherent state of expressing emotion, and trailed his fingertips along the sides of her waist to the sides of her breasts, and was rewarded by her slight moan. Shifting, peppering her lips with openmouthed kisses, he took the soft mound of flesh in his hand, luxuriating in the satiny softness of her skin and grazing his thumb over her nipple, preparing it for further attention. When he moved away from her mouth, kissing his way down her neck to her breast, it began to dawn on him that they really were going to make love, that she wasn't going to stop him, and she'd never done this before.

Something like panic and fear overwhelmed him, not because he was afraid that she didn't love him, but because he was afraid she loved him without knowing all the facts. The sense of fairness his father had ingrained in him from the age of two reared its ugly head and he stilled one millimeter above a hard, tempting nipple.

He squeezed his eyes shut.

If she wasn't a virgin he wouldn't need to hold this debate right now; the stakes wouldn't be so high, the consequences so dire. But she was a virgin and he couldn't make this decision for her.

Chapter Eight

Claire felt Evan stop and every nerve ending in her body froze. They were back to whatever it was that kept him from her. She knew it. She could hear the wheels of his mind turning. Whatever it was about her that he didn't like, or that he couldn't reconcile with himself or his life, it was bedeviling him again.

"Are you going to tell me about this, or am I going to live my life wondering why I'm not good enough for you?"

When he looked at her, his eyes were haunted. The cool, sophisticated expression he could muster to protect himself was long gone. And when he spoke, Claire felt as if she were talking to a stranger.

"You're probably better than I deserve."

"But..." Claire said, grabbing his wrist, refusing to let him move away from her when he tried. She wasn't ready to have him leave her. She wasn't ready for him to move away, for his emotions to pull back and his mind to start making excuses. Because in her estimation, the things that kept them apart were only that: excuses.

"The first time I kissed you, you stopped me and more or less told me we couldn't have a relationship because of the differences in our life-styles. Have you changed your mind about that?" he asked solemnly.

She took a slow, shallow breath, grateful that his reasoning was something she could handle. "Yes. Because I see how much alike we are. Don't you think that our similarities override our differences?"

"Yes and no," he admitted, and this time he did slip his wrist from her grip. "But I still see the differences."

Knowing she'd lost the battle the minute he moved away, Claire wept inside. She couldn't convince him if he continually erected walls. And he'd never let her get through to him if he wouldn't let her touch him. When he rolled off the sofa and handed her her blouse, Claire knew he hadn't merely moved physically, but emotionally, as well.

He paced away from her, sliding into his shirt and combing his fingers through his disheveled sandy brown hair. "Claire, we're very different in one important way."

"And that is?" she asked softly.

"You're still a virgin."

"And you're not?" she asked with mock surprise. "I'm shocked."

"This isn't funny. It's a problem for me."

"Oh."

Obviously hearing her disappointment, he raked his fingers through his hair again. "I don't mean to say you shouldn't have saved yourself for the right man.

I'm just saying there's no point in giving yourself to a man who might not be the right man.''

Knowing it was risky, knowing it was potentially humiliating, Claire whispered, "I think you are the right man."

He sighed heavily. "You don't really know me well enough to make that decision."

"And I won't ever get to know you if you keep talking in circles."

"All right, then, let me just get to the point." He turned, faced her again and caught her gaze. "Claire, you're young. You're innocent. And whether you like to admit it or not, you've hardly lived yet. I can't in good conscience ask you to commit to me. And I know that you don't want anything to do with sex unless the relationship will be permanent."

He stopped long enough to look at his bare feet, then carefully, sadly said, "At this point, I can't promise that it will be."

She had no way of knowing that what he was really telling her was that once she knew the truth *she* might be the one who wanted out. He could see she didn't even suspect that, because she had a wounded, disillusioned expression in her eyes.

Good, he thought, striding out of the room before he contradicted himself or, worse yet, told her the truth so she'd stop hurting. He didn't necessarily want her to hurt, but he wanted her to think…long and hard. Because he wasn't perfect, and if, after giving this more than passing consideration, she felt the same way that she felt now, he would explain everything to her. But he wanted her to be prepared for the truth when he told her. He needed to make damned sure she didn't commit to something without ample thought.

What he was doing right now was saving them grief and pain.

Sure, he thought, jogging up the steps when he heard Annie cry. He'd really saved both of them a lot of pain.

"I've been thinking that we might have better luck with our ad if we stopped advertising for a nanny and tried to find a housekeeper," Evan said.

Claire glanced over at Evan, who was sorting laundry, and she smiled. He was ankle-deep in little T-shirts, miniature blue jeans, tiny socks, ruffled-bottom tights and frilly dresses. A blue stripe of liquid detergent from their last attempt at washing clothes decorated the white washer. Cobwebs were forming in the corners of the usually tidy laundry room.

"I think you might be on to something."

"You're the one who said our biggest stumbling block to finding help was that most people realized they couldn't care for three babies at once. Well, Chas, Grant and I probably could, as long as we don't have to handle the housework, too."

"And chances are you could find someone willing to handle the cleaning, as long as they don't have to care for the babies."

"Precisely."

"I say we go for it."

"Great," Evan said, stepping over the sorted piles of dirty clothes. "You draft the ad first thing tomorrow morning."

"Okay," Claire agreed, following him out of the small utility room.

As always he looked sexy and adorable in his blue jeans and T-shirt. She loved the way he went barefoot around the house, let his hair fall into his eyes, and stretched out on the sofa when they were alone, comfortable in the intimate way of longtime lovers. Of course, there was nothing about him she didn't love, and she wondered about the oddness of that emotion when silly, preposterous things that were supposed to have nothing to do with romance, like laundry, could take her breath away.

It had been an entire week since the episode on the sofa, and in that time both Grant and Chas had returned, and left again. Chas had another interview with a different law firm, this one in Pittsburgh. Grant's partner, Grant had explained, was going through a messy divorce and was spending all of his time gathering data and preparing his testimony for a settlement hearing to assure that Grant didn't end up with a third partner in his construction company.

Chas had driven to Pittsburgh that afternoon and Grant had left for the airport only ten minutes before. Evan and Claire were alone again, but Claire didn't have any qualms. She loved being alone with him. She lived for the moment when the kids fell asleep and she and Evan had time to themselves. And she knew intuitively that Evan did, too.

She'd understood perfectly what Evan had been trying to tell her Friday night. He hadn't been rejecting her, as had been her first impression. What he had done was warn her that she needed to be very sure before they made any decisions.

Well, she was sure.

She hadn't needed the week. She hadn't even really needed a weekend to realize that even if there was an unhappy romance in his past, a child by a former lover or a crime that he'd committed, she would follow him to the ends of the earth anyway. Not because he was sexy, but because of his fairness, strength and intelligence at the mill, the way he fed the babies, the way he rocked and cuddled and coddled those kids, and, of course, the laundry. What woman could resist a man who had gorgeous green eyes, a perfect backside, hair that felt like silk and who didn't mind doing laundry? Whatever his problem, it was part of his past. A dead issue. Something they'd laugh about twenty years from now.

The only thing she hadn't really decided was how to tell him she'd made up her mind. She couldn't say she'd reconciled herself to a romance, child or crime from his past, because she didn't actually know the problem. And she couldn't go the seduction route, either. She might not have needed the week that followed their near miss on the couch to decide she loved him, but the distance had been necessary to make her see that she'd almost thrown away her biggest ideal— saving herself for marriage. She supposed what she had finally deduced was that they shouldn't be considering a sexual commitment, but a real commitment.

Given that Evan had gone to the extremes he had to force her to be certain she knew what she was doing before she took another step toward a relationship with him, Claire believed he cared as much for her as she cared for him—which meant they should be getting married, not contemplating sex.

The only problem was she didn't have a clue how to bring all this up with him.

"What do you say we play cards tonight?" Evan

asked as they walked through the kitchen and into the foyer on their way to the family room.

"We played cards last night," Claire replied distractedly.

In the end she concluded that what she had to do was ask him to marry her. If nothing else, a marriage proposal would get them talking about the subject he'd been skillfully dodging all week.

"TV, then?"

Oh, that would be terrific for mood, Claire thought, and wished she hadn't so quickly refused cards. With cards she would have had something to occupy her hands, something to look at in case his eyes saw too much, and a way to distract them if she lost her nerve.

When she didn't answer, Evan stopped suddenly. He pivoted and faced her so quickly she almost ran into him. "So what do you want to do, then?" he asked, exasperated.

Marry you, she thought and nearly said it. *I want to marry you, you big idiot.* She almost said that, too, but bit her tongue.

"Cards, TV, Scrabble," Evan said. "Our choices are very limited, Claire. This shouldn't be a difficult decision." He paused, considered, then said, "Unless you're really tired and you'd like to go home."

"No!" she shouted, nerves and panic getting the best of her. She lowered her voice and added, "TV would be fine."

She decided on television because this way she could sit beside him on the couch. Last Friday, they'd been watching TV, inching together, radiating attraction and sexual energy. If she could repeat that mood, if she could get him to admit through his actions that he wanted her, then she could easily ask him to marry her.

"Television," she repeated solemnly.

"Sure. Fine. Whatever," Evan said, turning away from her and leading her into the family room. He took a seat on the thick-cushioned recliner and Claire's eyes widened with dismay. She stared at him for about thirty seconds, wondering how she could re-create a mood when he wasn't cooperating, then she remembered that they'd been sharing a bowl of popcorn and that's why they had been sitting side by side.

"You know what," she said abruptly, nervously wringing her hands. "I think I'm going to make popcorn."

Evan snapped his recliner down again. "I'll help."

For a few seconds Claire considered telling him he didn't need to help, but she wanted him off the recliner enough that she was willing to have him follow her into the kitchen and get in her way while she performed the uncomplicated task of microwaving popcorn. Who knew? Maybe she'd get an opportunity to pop the question while she was popping corn.

She wrung her hands again. "Okay. Yeah. You can help."

He frowned at her. "Is something wrong?"

"No. No. I'm fine."

Narrow-eyed, he bent close to take a good look at her face. "You don't look fine." His frown deepened. "I think you should go home."

"I'm fine," she said, nerves making her voice much, much firmer than necessary. She led him back to the kitchen, scolding herself for sniping at him when she was supposed to be preparing him for a marriage proposal. Then almost yelled at him again because every time she turned around he was in her way. Finally, he took the bag of popcorn from her hands, directed her to one of the stools by the counter and tossed the little bag into the microwave himself.

"I'm sorry," she apologized miserably.

"That's all right," he said kindly. "You're tired. I understand."

Claire sighed heavily. "No, I don't think you do."

"Then why don't you explain it to me?"

That was a fine idea. In fact, it was the perfect idea and perfect timing, and the perfect introduction.

Folding her hands together to still them, she took a long breath and said, "Evan, all this week I've been thinking—"

"Hey, anybody home?" Grant called as he entered the back door. "I forgot my carry-on bag."

He had a strange look on his face as if he called out to them because he was afraid he might be interrupting something. Evan angrily scowled at his brother, but Claire only stared at him in defeat.

"It will take me two minutes to run upstairs and get it," he said as he strode through the room, "then I'll be on my way again."

"You know, Grant, since you're here," Evan said, following him out of the room, "I might as well tell you that Claire and I decided that rather than advertise for a nanny, we should try advertising for a housekeeper."

"Hey, that's a great idea," Grant replied, his voice trailing off as he walked farther away from the kitchen.

Claire sagged on her stool. That was an opportunity that would never come again. It had been perfectly timed. They were alone. The kids were sleeping soundly. She knew what she wanted to say and Evan was listening. With triplets and two brothers, a chance like that would probably come along once, and Claire had missed it.

The sound of footfalls pounding down the steps rolled into the kitchen a minute before the two Brewsters did. The microwave beeped, announcing the completion of her popcorn. Grant strode to the door, opened it, said, "Bye, Claire," and was gone.

Before Claire had a chance to get any more nervous, the sound of silence enveloped her.

Evan reached for the popcorn.

Claire licked her dry lips. Should she—could she—return them to those few seconds before Grant bounded into the room?

She had to.

"Evan, I..."

He looked up. "That's right. You were just about to tell me something, weren't you?"

She sighed with relief. "Actually, I was going to ask you something."

He gave her a solemn look. "Sounds serious."

"It is. It's serious and important."

"And requires my complete attention?"

"Yes."

"Okay, let's have it, then."

"All right," she said, and cleared her throat. "Evan, the way I see this..."

The shrill ring of the telephone interrupted her and Claire slumped with disappointment.

"That's okay. You go ahead and talk. We'll just let it ring."

Claire drew a breath, trying to recapture her focus and concentration, but the phone rang again.

"Don't pay any attention to that. You go ahead."

"Well, I..." she began again, trying to ignore the phone, which seemed to be ringing more quickly and more loudly than ever before.

"Talk," Evan said. "It can't be important. Who could be calling us...except Chas," he said, remembering. "He's always in trouble, Claire. I'm sorry. I'd better get this."

Frustrated and nervous, Claire wandered out of the room as he grabbed the phone. That was it. If a brotherly interruption and a ringing phone weren't signs from God that she shouldn't propose, then Claire didn't know what was. Realizing she'd forgotten the popcorn, she turned, stalked back to the kitchen, snatched the bowl and marched out again.

Less than a minute later, Evan joined her in the family room. He sat beside her on the sofa and Claire thought sourly that she'd gotten exactly what she wanted, simply at the wrong time and when she was definitely out of the mood.

"All right. Now, what did you want?"

She sighed. "Nothing."

"Oh, come on. I know it was something. Not only did it make you nervous, but the interruptions upset you. So, I know it's something and I know it's important."

"Frankly, right at this minute, I'm wondering about my sanity for even considering what I was going to ask you."

"Now you have me curious."

"Well, you'll stay curious."

"Claire," Evan said, but it was more of a groan. "Come on. I couldn't help that we were interrupted."

Claire sighed. "And I can't help that I lost my nerve. So, let's just forget it, all right?"

"No. I'm not going to forget it, because if you don't tell me, I'm going to feel guilty all night for something I didn't do."

Ignoring him, Claire reached for the remote and clicked on a new channel. When she returned the remote to the coffee table, she set the popcorn beside it because she had only wanted popcorn to get Evan on the sofa with her. Now he was seated beside her, obviously willing to listen, and she felt like an idiot.

"Out with it," Evan said in a slow, seductive voice.

Feeling young, humiliated and embarrassed, Claire shook her head. "Evan, please, could we forget this?"

"No. If it was important to you, it's important to me, too."

Because she really wanted to believe that, she peeked at him.

He smiled hopefully.

When she still didn't say anything, he said, "You know, if you don't tell me, I'm not going to have any choice but to tickle it out of you."

Her eyes widened. "You wouldn't."

"I would," he said, his fingers making contact with her ribs and tickling mercilessly.

Claire squealed and tried to slide away from him, but he was too quick for her. He caught her arm and yanked her back. They tussled and wrestled for what seemed like forever, with Claire laughing and trying to twist away and Evan proving both his superior strength and his sense of humor.

But as quickly as he'd started tickling her, he stopped. Because she needed to catch her breath, it took Claire a minute before she realized that he'd stopped tickling because they were sprawled out on the couch, Evan pinning her down with the full length of his body.

Her gaze shot to his. Mesmerized, she stared into his beautiful emerald eyes, reminding herself that this might be the perfect moment to propose, but too spellbound by his hypnotizing gaze to actually form the words.

His eyes lowered and he glanced at her mouth. The internal debate she knew was taking place left her breathless with anticipation and trepidation. She'd learned her lesson about pushing him into things. If he kissed her it had to be his idea. He had to want to. He had to want it as much as she wanted it.

Seconds tormentingly ticked by, then slowly, deliberately, he brought his lips to hers.

First he nibbled the corners, then traced the shape with his tongue. Claire didn't move. She didn't even breathe. Part of her worried that any sort of response from her might break the spell, ruin the moment. Another part was spiraling into a languorous heaven where only emotion and sensation existed. She could feel every inch of him pressed against every inch of her, even as he made absolute, devoted, sensual love to her mouth.

While she fell into an arousal-induced haze, it dawned on Claire that the perfect moment had finally arrived. His desire proved he wanted her, the care he took showed he loved her. If she asked him to marry her now, he wouldn't be able to lie about his feelings.

"Evan," she whispered as his lips brushed against hers.

"Yes," he answered softly.

"Evan, will you marry me?"

Chapter Nine

Evan froze. The forbidden hope that she wanted him forever sprang up in him before he could stop it, drowning out the fear that the truth would send her away for good. At first he couldn't say anything. Couldn't move. He savored everything he was feeling because he knew that this moment came only once in every man's life. A surge of wonder filled him. Then a blessed sense of rightness enveloped him. Then gratitude, joy…euphoria. Evan experienced all the things he had always suspected a man would feel when the woman he loved told him she wanted to spend her life with him, to give him her heart, to give him her mornings, her Christmases, her love for the rest of her life.

He let the sensations wash over him. He let them cuddle his heart. He let himself know and understand what it felt like to be normal, then he squeezed his eyes shut, swallowed hard and pulled himself away from Claire before she had the chance to hold him.

"Claire, you can't marry me," he said abruptly, shattering the passion-sprinkled atmosphere.

Clever, astute, Claire said, "We're not talking about me and what I can and can't do. *I* asked *you* to marry me. What's *your* answer?"

"I'd marry you in a New York minute," he replied without a second's hesitation. "I'd try to make you the happiest woman in the world and I'd love you like you've never been loved before."

He could see his response took her breath away, boggled her into speechlessness. Before she regained coherent thought and attempted to argue him out of his right decision, he added, "But I can't, Claire. I can't have children. And all I have to do is take one look at you with the triplets and I know you were born to have your own children."

Poised to dispute whatever he said, Claire stopped her immediate denial a split second before she would have made it. "You can't have children?" she whispered, stunned, then realized that was the only rationale for his behavior that made any sense. It explained why he so desperately wanted the triplets. Why he treated them just slightly different from the way his brothers treated them. It explained why he pulled away from her when they both knew he was drawn to her.

It explained why she couldn't marry him.

She swallowed. "I don't know what to say."

"And I appreciate your honesty," Evan said, pacing away from the sofa to the television, which he manually silenced.

In a deluge of desolate wisdom, Claire understood that he was telling her he appreciated that she hadn't hotly denied that this would make any difference.

What he didn't know was that she was going through emotions so rapidly she almost couldn't keep up with them. She'd never had a moment of happiness annihilated so quickly. But confusion had been replaced by fury at the unfairness of it all, and a horrible sense of relief that he'd been strong enough, man enough to admit the truth to her before they had passed a point of no return.

The fury she could deal with. Every person had a right to a sense of injustice at loss.

The relief shamed her.

"I'm so sorry," she said, studying him as he stood by the cold fireplace. He looked alone and forlorn, his silky hair tipped to his forehead, his serious green eyes staring at the empty hearth. Her love for him resonated through her body. She wanted nothing more than to go to him and comfort him.

But common sense and logic forced her to stay where she was. Other things he'd said began to fall into place. His warnings took on new meaning. Could she live her life without children of her own? Would the triplets be enough? Would she selfishly change her mind about insisting Evan's brothers be involved in raising the triplets? How would she handle *never* being anyone's biological mother? Never seeing her own expression in another person's eyes? Never hearing her voice come from a smaller version of herself? Never hearing a giggle that might be an echo of her own childish laugh? Could she live without knowing the joy of pregnancy or the sacrifice of giving birth? Could she make hundreds of choices about her entire life in one decision?

Could anyone?

"I think it's best to go, Claire," Evan said softly, quietly.

She swallowed hard. How could she leave him alone now?

"You're too young to make these kinds of commitments and choices."

Agreed. She knew that was part of the problem.

"And I'm too old to wait for you to make up your mind. Particularly since you'd have every right in the world to choose your maternal needs over the very fragile, very precarious love of one man."

"Evan, this is all so sudden. You've just given me surprising, difficult news," she said rationally. "I am going to go home," she admitted as she rose. "But I'll be back tomorrow and we'll talk about this."

As if the devil had pushed him, he spun to face her. The hurt in his eyes told her that the pain she felt at the injustice of it all was only a fraction of his. "You just don't get it, do you? I don't want to talk about this. I don't want a woman to have to make huge sacrifices for me. I don't want anyone to sacrifice for me. If you have to think about it, it's not right. *We're* not right."

"But..."

"Please go."

Claire drew in a shuddering breath. She knew exactly what he was telling her. Love wasn't necessarily supposed to be easy, but certain things were supposed to be automatic. And he was also right about something else.

She wasn't going to change her mind. Her maternal instincts were too strong. Her needs, her wants, the mental pictures she'd carried around since her days of playing house as a child—they all included babies. *Her* babies.

"I'm sorry," she said, then pivoted and ran from the room, cursing life, cursing everything.

"I can't believe you turned down another job."

Though having anyone speak in the deadly silence of the dinner table should have been a blessing, Evan knew his statement to Chas actually made the strained atmosphere even thicker.

But Chas only shrugged. "It wasn't right for me."

Hoping he could find a way or means to change the subject he shouldn't have broached, Evan harnessed his anger and looked around the dining room. All three babies had been fed and were seated in high chairs behind their brothers. Each entertained himself or herself with a plastic toy. Grant had assumed his rightful place at the head of the table. Claire was in her usual chair, but Evan had chosen to sit beside Chas rather than Claire.

He'd thought it was a good move because he didn't want to be beside her, inadvertently hinting that they were a pair. But in the four days since he'd made this decision, he'd come to regret it, because now every day at mealtime he was forced to look at her and see the beauty that had attracted him to her as well as her obvious regret.

God, he hated the regret. It made him want to make promises he knew he couldn't keep. It made him want to beg her to make sacrifices that weren't fair.

"I just don't think I'm cut out for a big law firm."

"Or a six-figure salary," Evan said curtly, so swamped in his own unhappiness that he couldn't seem to stop himself, though he knew he should. "You keep forgetting that you're in debt, Chas."

"How could I possibly forget anything when I have you here to constantly remind me?" Chas countered, tossing his linen napkin to the table. "For the past four days you have done nothing but pick at me for this and I'm tired of it."

"All I'm saying is that you could have taken the job for a year or so, gotten yourself out of debt and moved on with the rest of your life."

"You know what, Evan?" Chas said, rising from his seat. "I'm sorry I'm not like you and Grant. I'm sorry I don't see the future as easily and clearly as the two of you do. I'm sorry I'm not perfect. But I'm not. I'm broke. I'm already divorced—twice. I'm probably never going to find the right woman, and I'll never have the 2.5 perfect kids that you and Grant undoubtedly will have."

Chas began to stride to the door, but Claire mentally gasped and her gaze jumped to Evan, who hadn't even reacted. Recognizing Chas would have never been so cruel deliberately, and that even if he could be, Grant wouldn't let him, she realized Evan's brothers didn't know his secret.

"That's enough out of both of you," Grant said sternly. "Chas, get back here and finish your dinner."

"No. I'm sick of…"

"That's all right," Evan said quietly. "You stay, Chas. I'll leave."

"There is no reason for either of you to leave," Grant thundered.

"Yeah, and who died and made you Dad?" Evan countered angrily, but the second the words were out of his mouth, the dining room became deadly quiet.

Evan shook his head, slammed his napkin to his plate and bounded out of the room.

Grant sighed heavily. "I give up," he said, and he also left the room.

Chas looked at the door, then glanced at the three happy babies gurgling and chewing on their plastic toys, and back at Claire.

"Don't stay on my account," she urged gently. "You go. Go jog, go read, go watch television or have a beer. Do whatever it is you do to blow off steam. I'll take care of the kids."

"There are three kids here, Claire," Chas said, but he swallowed. "You need help."

"No, you need a break. You go."

He gave her a helpless look. "You're sure?"

"I'm positive. I've handled the kids before..."

As she said the last, Evan returned, shoving into the dining room through the swinging door with a little more force than was necessary.

"Go," Claire commanded Chas.

He nodded and left the room.

"Coddling my brothers again?" Evan asked the second Chas was out of earshot.

"Guess what, Evan?" Claire said incredulously. "You and your brothers suffered a great loss recently, and you were thrown a tremendous challenge. You all deserve to be coddled a little. There are very few people in this world who could be handed three babies and take it in stride. If there's tension in this house, it's normal. If I try to help alleviate it, that only means..."

"That you had a great deal of respect for our father and you're a very good person," Grant put in from the doorway. "Evan, take a break," he ordered. "Claire, go home. *I* will handle the kids."

"But…" Claire persisted.

"I'm not taking orders…" Evan began at the same time.

"Enough!" Grant roared. "Here's the deal. Chas and I have been out of town more than we've been in town in the past two weeks. Both of you need a break. I'm giving it to you. Now go. Better yet, go together. Go to a movie. Go to the diner and get pie. Just go."

Claire drew in a deep breath. "Maybe he's right," she said softly. "Would you like to see a movie?"

Furious, Evan squeezed his eyes shut. "I don't want to do *anything* with you," he said, then stormed out of the room.

Grant rubbed his hands down his face and sighed heavily. "Now I finally see what happened. You two had a fight, didn't you. That's why he's been a bear and you've been quieter than a church mouse."

"We didn't have a fight," Claire denied sadly.

"Oh, yeah, right. And I'm not six foot three."

"We really didn't," Claire said, gathered her dirty dishes, carried them to the kitchen, and silently left through the back door.

"I'm sorry," Evan apologized to Claire as he stepped out of the elevator the next morning.

Claire sighed. "I think Grant was right. I think we all just need a break."

"So, do you want me to take you to the movies?"

Claire smiled and shook her head. "No."

Evan nodded. "I didn't think so," he said, and turned and walked away from her.

"I didn't mean that the way you obviously took it," Claire objected, following him into his office.

Evan removed his suit coat, hung it in the closet and made his way back to his desk. "Whatever."

"Don't you see I…"

Evan shook his head. "Don't you see? I don't want to talk about this." Miserable, he fell into his chair. "We've made our choices. Now let's move on without belaboring the issue."

"I don't think it's belaboring an issue to want to talk about it."

"I do," Evan said, then promptly occupied himself with work, cutting her off.

Claire nearly contradicted him and insisted they discuss this, but in the end she decided against it. First, she'd made her decision. He was right. There was nothing else to discuss. She couldn't reconcile herself to a life without children. Second, if she wasn't going to marry him, then she couldn't be a close enough confidante to share this burden with him. That privilege was reserved for a special person.

Now she understood why he'd first chosen Abby. She wished miserably that she would have stayed out of that, but knew in her heart that Abby probably would have had the same problem with Evan that she was having. Given that there was no easy way out of this, Claire quietly left the room and mimicked Evan's plan. She plunged herself so far into work that she didn't have time to think about the injustices of life or how much it hurt to lose the person you loved by your own choosing.

That night after Claire and Evan had bathed the babies, Evan took charge of Taylor and dressed her in a lightweight one-piece pink sleeper. Though Claire was busy putting Cody into his pajamas, something about the interaction between Evan and the baby drew her attention, and she watched as he carried the little girl to the rocker. As casually and naturally as if he were Taylor's real father, Evan smoothed his lips over the crown of her head as he positioned her to take a bottle before bed. He nestled the child against his chest, leaned back in the rocker and peacefully closed his eyes.

Her love for him sneaked up on her before she could stop it. The warm joyful feeling streaked through her, leaving her almost breathless. Rationally, she knew that one of the things that attracted her to this man was that she'd unconsciously put him into the role of the father of her own children. Every display of love he made toward the triplets only served to remind her that he personified every trait she envisioned. Except he couldn't be the father of her children. He couldn't be the father of anyone's children.

Reminding herself of the bitter truth, Claire waited for the wash of regret, but it never came. Instead, she felt only deep respect, admiration and tenderness for him. On the heels of those came the attraction. The desire to touch him. The desire to kiss him, to hold him, to belong to him.

After carrying the baby to the rocker, Claire allowed herself to close her eyes and wonder again what it might have been like to belong to him. To be his equal. His friend. His lover. To share his life in a way no other person would. The sensations stirred by her imaginings were so deep and so primitive, Claire knew she had to stop her fantasies. She couldn't have this man. Not on her terms. Not necessarily on terms he'd chosen, either. But terms dictated by fate. Because fate decreed that he not have children, but also ordained that she desperately want children, she had to recognize that could only mean fate did not want them together.

Which meant she had to stop thinking about things like this.

But when she opened her eyes it was to find Evan watching her.

"Cody's out like a light," he whispered, nodding toward the sleeping baby.

Without realizing she was doing it, Claire studied the deep green of Evan's eyes, the angle of his cheekbones, the curve of the lock of hair that fell to his forehead. He was unbearably handsome to her. The epitome of sexy. The embodiment of perfection.

Finally recognizing she was staring, she cleared her throat. "I guess I'd better put him in the crib, then."

Evan smiled. "I guess you'd better. I'll meet you downstairs."

When he was gone Claire sagged against the rocker, wondering if he could read her mind. She reprimanded herself for thinking foolish things, dragging them to a place where they couldn't go and in general making things more difficult.

But when she ventured into the family room, Evan didn't seem at all displeased with her. Having her stare at him didn't appear to have affected him at all. If anything, he was inordinately obliging.

"I made you popcorn and I also brought in some chips. No matter what you want, it's here," he said cheerfully as she took a seat on the sofa.

"Thanks," she said, and changed her mind about apologizing for behaving like a silly schoolgirl upstairs, if only because he was acting so normally and seemed so much happier than he had for the past week that she didn't want to break the mood.

His good nature held up well enough that by the end of the night Claire was wondering if *she* wasn't the one with the problem. Maybe he wasn't as attracted to her as she thought. Maybe she'd taken the wrong meaning from things he'd said and done.

Claire realized that he might not have been as affected by the loss as she was. She also recognized that if he could handle being together sixteen hours a day and not only be pleasant but be friendly, then she would have to be able to do the same thing.

But the next day after discovering Evan had hired a secretary and pretending all day that it didn't hurt her not to be consulted, Claire was positive she'd misinterpreted his feelings for her and worked twice as hard to pretend she was unaffected and happy. But when she got behind the wheel of her car, and Evan was sure everyone was out of the executive suite, both slumped in their seats. But just as quickly, they remembered it was Grant and Chas's night out and pasted on a happy smile. Though they marveled at the sheer strength of will required, each was determined that the other would never see how much this hurt.

Chapter Ten

"Are you sure everything is okay?" Grant asked, stepping into the nursery.

Claire looked up from diapering Annie. "Yeah, we're fine. Aren't we, Annie?"

The baby gurgled with happiness, but Grant frowned. "I'm not talking about you and the babies."

"Everything's fine at the mill, too."

"I'm not talking about the mill."

Claire only stared at him for a second. "Then what are you talking about?"

"You and Evan. Is it okay to leave the two of you alone?"

"Of course," Claire said, then she laughed, not because she thought the situation was funny, but because she knew Grant felt she and Evan were having some sort of battle. The easiest way to make him believe things were fine was to laugh. So she laughed.

Grant sighed. "Boy, that's a relief. What the hell did you two fight about, anyway?"

"We didn't actually fight," Claire replied. She knew she couldn't tell him the whole story, but she also recognized Grant wasn't going to drop the issue unless she gave him some sort of explanation. "We sort of had a difference of opinion."

"That's a fight, Claire."

"Not really," Claire said, then slid Annie into pajamas. "I like to think of it as spirited debate."

Grant shook his head and started to walk out of the room. "It's no wonder my father liked you," he said, slipping into the hall, closing the door behind him.

But when he was gone, Claire frowned. If Grant felt the need to ask if everything was okay, then she wasn't doing a very good job of hiding her feelings. Particularly since Evan was much more astute about her and her emotions than either of his brothers. If Grant suspected something was wrong, then Evan would soon notice, too. And she couldn't have that. Evan had enough on his mind. He didn't need to worry about her feelings.

To protect Evan's privacy—so his brothers didn't poke and prod and try to get to the bottom of a problem Evan apparently wasn't ready to share—and also to hide her broken heart, Claire obviously had to be much happier than she was pretending.

Evan thought exactly the same thing after Grant checked in on him. He knew Grant was a worrier, but he also recognized that Grant was an observant man. To protect Claire's privacy over the choices she'd made, and also to protect her from *his* broken heart, he had to be much more convincing that none of this bothered him.

When he heard Claire running down the steps, he

scooted out into the hall, Cody in his arms. "My turn," he said cheerfully, indicating that he would be carrying Cody up to the bathtub now that the girls were taken care of.

Smiling brightly, Claire tickled Cody under the chin and was rewarded with a bubbly giggle. "You be a good boy," she said, and stepped out of the way so Evan could climb the stairs.

"He's the best boy, aren't you, Cody?"

"Yes, he is. Cody is the best boy," Claire called after them, but when Evan had finished the climb up the steps and started down the hall, she sagged with relief.

She never realized how tiring happiness could be.

Evan found her in the family room about half an hour later. "All three are asleep," he announced merrily. "So what would you like to do? Cards? Television? Scrabble?"

What she wanted to do was curl up in a chair, or maybe go to sleep early, here, rather than make the long drive to her apartment. Instead, she smiled. "Scrabble would be fun."

"Great," Evan enthused. "I'll get some pretzels. You set up the game."

Claire refused herself a heavy sigh when he left. She couldn't give in to the urge to voice her sorrow every time she was alone. If she was ever going to get back to normal again, it would only be through disciplining herself to get beyond these feelings of loss. So, when he returned, Claire had the game pieces distributed and was seated in her chair, ready to begin.

They played for only ten minutes before Evan said, "Claire, I don't think *humbug* is a real word."

Tired, annoyed, Claire barely checked the impulse

to narrow her eyes at him. She fortified herself with a quick, quiet breath and cheerfully said, "Of course, it is."

"I think we should look it up," Evan said, smiling at her.

She returned his smile, though behind it, her teeth were gritted. "You're challenging me?"

His smile became a grin. "I guess I am."

Claire had never known anyone who could be so insulting and look so happy about it. Her anger built as he strode to the bookshelves and rummaged for the dictionary, but as she watched him from behind, her irritation quickly waned. When she recognized that was because she was staring at the long length of his back, his cute derriere and his sturdy thighs, she almost groaned with disappointment at herself and her inability to be mature about this. Luckily, he pivoted and grinned at her again. "*Humbug* isn't in here."

"Oh, yeah, right," she said, springing from her seat. "It's got to be in there. They say it eight thousand times in *A Christmas Carol*."

"You've counted?" Evan asked cockily.

This time she allowed herself the pleasure of narrowing her eyes. "Haven't you ever heard of hyperbole?"

"Touchy," Evan said, and handed her the dictionary. He strode back to the table, getting away from her the very second the opportunity presented itself.

He wouldn't allow himself any sort of acknowledgment of the effect she was having on him, but he did sneak his hand across the back of his neck. He loved it when she was snippy. He couldn't believe it had ever annoyed him. She was an intelligent, vibrant woman, and when she was angry, she was magnificent, passionate. *Passionate.* That's what she was. That's what he loved about her. Her zest for life. Her passion. He couldn't even begin to wonder what it would be like to make love...

He stopped his musings and ran his hand across the back of his neck again.

That train of thought wasn't going to get him anywhere but into trouble.

"Humbug," she said, and thrust the dictionary under his nose. *"H-u-m-b-u-g."*

Smelling her cologne, Evan almost closed his eyes. Instead he focused them on the page to which she pointed. "That's *hamburg.*"

"Damn it, it is not. It's *humbug.*"

"I'm telling you it's *hamburg.*"

"And I'm telling you, you need glasses."

As if they simultaneously realized they were being ridiculous, both stepped back a pace.

"Sorry."

"Sorry."

"Take the points for *humbug.* I'll take the loss for an incorrect challenge."

"No. I'll take my *humbug* points, but you can forget the challenge."

"No..."

"Stop it," she yelped, throwing up her hands. "Could we just play the stupid game without being so damned polite to each other?"

Evan decided it was best not to pursue that and again took his seat. Claire also sat and began pulling new tiles to replace the ones she'd used.

"Just for the record," she murmured, *"humbug* is a word."

"I didn't see it," he replied, equally quiet, equally casual.

"That's because you weren't looking."

"I looked exactly where your finger pointed."

"Baloney. You didn't look. Lately, you stay seven feet away from anything that has to do with me."

"More hyperbole?"

"No, that one's fact."

He sighed, as if ready to reply, but she stopped him with a wave of her hand. "No. Save it. I don't want to get into an argument."

"Claire, we've been arguing since you put down the tiles for *humbug.* So quit trying to pretend that we're not. Or that you're above that," he added snidely.

She glared at him. "And what the hell is that supposed to mean?"

Unable to stop himself, Evan rose to pace. "Just what I said. You have an annoying tendency to be happy about everything."

"Oh, and what would you like me to do? Get angry every twenty minutes? Argue with your orders at work?"

"Actually, I sort of liked it when you argued with my orders at work. At least," he said, "I knew you were being honest."

Infuriated, she grabbed his elbow and spun him around. It was on the tip of her tongue to remind him that if she was pretending anything, it was for his benefit. Besides, if anyone wasn't showing his true feelings, it was him. "At least I didn't have to hire a secretary to protect myself."

His eyes widened in disbelief. "I hired a secretary to take some of the workload off you."

"Baloney."

She turned to go, but he grabbed her arm to stop her. The second his fingers touched her soft, supple flesh, every bit of irritation he felt, every bit of frustration he felt melted. He knew he had every right in the world to be angry and tired, but he also knew that it wasn't Claire's fault and he shouldn't be taking it out on her. Unfortunately, he also knew he was only taking it out on her because he wanted her. That was the biggest thing he remembered when he touched her. That he wanted her. When her smooth, soft skin slid against his palms, a hundred sensations bombarded him. A hundred realizations hit him. A hundred wishes confronted him.

"This time I really am sorry," he whispered, and was gifted with the opportunity to look into her eyes because she gazed up at him.

He told himself to let go of her elbow, told himself to break the stare and take his seat. He did neither.

He watched the color of her eyes darken. He watched the shimmering blue clarity turn smoky and hazy with desire. He wished with all his heart that he could kiss her. Just one soft brush of his mouth against hers. Just a quick taste. That's all he really wanted. From the look in her eyes, he knew she wanted it, too, in spite of the fact that she was trying like hell not to. He suddenly, clearly knew that she'd been pretending a lot of things over the past two weeks, but just as suddenly, just as clearly, he also knew why.

The second he remembered why, he dropped her arm and stepped back a pace. "Why don't you go home?"

"No. Let's just finish the game."

He almost argued, but after another quick look into her eyes, he recognized what she was telling him. Nothing about their feelings had changed. Their situation might be dictating that they not act on those feelings, but the feelings themselves hadn't changed.

They had to live with them. They had to deal with them. And she was a much better, much stronger person than he was.

"So, Headlights ambles over, taps Chas on the shoulder and says, 'I think you and I have some unfinished business from a few years ago.'"

Claire listened with something akin to absolute panic as Grant laughingly told his story. Her heart was beating a hundred beats a second, her palms had begun to sweat. The last thing Chas needed was to get arrested two weeks before he found out if he passed the bar.

From her seat on the sofa, Claire watched as Evan slowly sank into his chair as if pulling back his temper, and she knew he felt exactly the same way she did.

"What did Chas do?" Evan asked quietly.

"He said, 'Headlights, you wanna hit me, you go ahead. But I think you better realize I'm a lawyer now. I don't fight with my fists, I fight with words. You hit me and that pretty red truck of yours will be sitting in my driveway before the end of the year.'"

Claire watched Evan relax as that information seemed to sink in by degrees. His gaze traveled to hers and they shared a second of complete relief.

Obviously noticing the exchanged look, Grant groaned. "Hey, did you think I'd come home and brag about the fact that he tore up the town?"

"No," Evan admitted with a long sigh. "I can see that you're just as concerned about him as Claire and I are."

"Okay, then," Grant said, pleased with himself. "I think the episode tonight means he's finally on the right track."

"Yeah, as long as we can keep him away from pretty girls..." Evan said, then he stole a glance at Claire. "Present company excluded."

"Aw, he knows she's taken anyway," Grant said, then rose from his seat in the den. "Well, I've had it for one day. I'm going to bed. Claire, it's so late I think you should stay here tonight. In fact, I'm surprised Evan didn't send you home hours ago."

Even as he said the words, Grant's eyes widened with understanding. "Oh," he said, walking out of the den. "Never mind."

Embarrassed because she knew exactly what Grant hinted at, Claire sat as still as she possibly could, not wanting to draw attention to herself as she waited for the self-consciousness to pass.

Evan did nothing for a few seconds, then kicked at her toe. "Sorry about that," he apologized quietly.

"That's okay."

"No, it's not. He doesn't know about my not being able to have kids, so he doesn't realize that you and I more or less put a stop to the attraction between us."

Not quite agreeing with the stop part, Claire nodded anyway. "So he figured you might have wanted me to stay..."

"To sleep with you," Evan agreed casually. "Men are pigs," he added, grinning at her.

Claire couldn't help it, she laughed. "Yeah, basically, as a group, I'm afraid I'm going to have to agree that you are."

"I'm glad you said 'as a group.'"

"That's because individually most of you are actually harmless."

Evan studied her for a second. "You think so?"

"Basically."

"You think I'm harmless?"

She knew the instant he said it that he wouldn't be. Not that he'd hurt her, but if they ever made love, he'd change her. She knew that for an absolute fact. And she wasn't entirely sure that was a good thing.

But she also knew that she'd begun her metamorphosis the minute she met him. Watching him as he sat smiling at her, she wondered about the generosity and goodness of a man who could so selflessly give up all the pleasures of love because he wouldn't tie a woman to him. As she thought that, her love for him seemed to grow again and she wondered who she was trying to kid—him or herself.

She loved him. He loved her. Just as she'd told him about Abby, it wouldn't be fair for her to marry another man. It wouldn't be fair to that man.

She had to marry *him*.

Somehow she had to come to terms with not having children, and then convince Evan to marry her. She had to find a way to make him see this was a sacrifice she was willing to make.

"So, run this by me again," Abby said as Claire sank into the thick sofa by the fireplace in what Abby called the living quarters of her family's bed-and-breakfast. It was Friday night, the night Claire usually left the Brewster brothers and their triplets to fend for themselves. After cocoa and two long stories, Tyler had been put to bed. Now Abby and Claire sat in the homey seating area.

"I have a friend from college who is considering marrying a man who can't have children," Claire said, and didn't feel the slightest bit guilty about the lie because she wouldn't violate Evan's privacy, but she also needed Abby's advice.

Abby threw her voluminous red hair over her shoulder. "So, what's her problem?"

Claire licked her suddenly dry lips. "Well, she'll never have her own children."

"I don't see why not."

At Abby's flippant attitude, Claire said, "You're missing the point here. Most women want to have kids."

"And as long as there is nothing wrong with your friend, I can't see why she won't have kids. In this day and age there are all kinds of technologies. Granted, she won't have her *husband's* children, but she can have children."

Claire had to admit she'd already considered that, but the conclusion she'd drawn wasn't a pleasant one. "Don't you think her husband would feel left out?"

Abby shrugged. "I think that would all depend on the guy. If he's some sort of egotist, he may not like the deal. But if he wants the best for his wife and wants to be a father, then he'll probably agree. How much does *he* want kids?"

"A lot," Claire replied absently, because she finally realized what was bothering her about the alternative technologies for producing children. Evan was a smart enough man that he should have thought of each and every one of them, but instead of offering her this solution, he'd more or less given up on loving her. Almost as if he'd been grabbing for an excuse to get out of their relationship.

Abby let Claire contemplate that for a few seconds, before she said, "Come on, out with it. I can see something about this is bothering you."

After drawing in a long breath, Claire said, "I guess I'm wondering why my friend's fiancé didn't think of this himself."

"Or maybe you're borrowing trouble," Abby suggested with a lilting laugh. "You do have a tendency to overanalyze everything."

"I know."

"This isn't a topic that's going to come up over breakfast cereal, Claire," Abby reminded her. "Or it could be that your friend's fiancé has brought it up and your friend just hasn't confided that end of it to you."

"No," Claire said, shaking her head. "He hasn't brought it up."

Abby thought about that for a second. "Maybe he hasn't brought it up because he wants *her* to think of it."

Claire stole a glance at her friend. "What do you mean?"

"It might be a test of some sort. If he brings it up and she agrees, then he'll never know if she's committed or if she compromised. But if she brings it up, he might see that as her way of committing to him. Just the fact that she went in search of an answer to their problem could be the proof he's looking for that she loves him." With that Abby sighed, then tossed a pillow at Claire. "Look who you're coming to for advice about men! For pete's sake, Claire, I lost the love of my life when I was eighteen and I've hardly dated since. I'm the last person anybody should come to for advice."

Tossing the pillow back at Abby, Claire laughed. "I keep forgetting you're not 'Dear Abby,'" she said, then nestled into the comfort of the sofa. Of course. Evan was testing her. He was always saying she was too young to commit, or pushing her away, or forcing her to think for herself—now she knew why! He wanted her to come up with this plan on her own— and she had, sort of.

"Actually, Abby, I wish I'd come to you sooner."

Thunderstorms were not exactly a rarity in Brewster County, but severe storms were. When the wind whipped through the trees with enough force to bend the branches almost to the ground, Evan started worrying. Chas, however, was asleep on the leather sofa and Grant was studying the computer printout of the profit and loss statement for the mill.

"I don't even see a ripple."

"Excuse me?" Evan said, turning away from the window to look at his older brother.

Grant grinned. "I don't even see a hint of a change in command. You've had the company over two months, but there isn't any way anyone would notice. Everything's exactly the same."

"Don't get too excited, Grant," Evan cautioned, then paced to another window to see if the view was different. He had an odd, uncomfortable feeling about this storm, about Claire, actually. And since it was storming, he decided that he must be worried she was driving in this. "First of all, the mill is an established business, our customers are something like friends who support us without question. It will be months before they realize Dad's not running the place anymore. And months before their loyalties begin to waiver."

"Oh, that's bull," Grant said with a dismissing wave of his hand. "Our customers stay with us because we provide good products."

"For now," Evan agreed absently. "But no one can predict the future."

"Lord, when in the hell did you become such a pessimist?"

Watching a particularly brilliant flash of lightning, Evan drew in a deep drink of air. "I'm not a pessimist. I'm a realist."

"No, you're a nut," Chas mumbled from his position on the leather sofa.

For a few seconds, Evan wondered if Chas was right. He had a strange, compelling feeling that something was wrong. Something big. Something critical. He almost wished the profit and loss statement had been a disaster because that would have explained this nagging sensation. But with the success of the switch in leadership at the mill, the babies safely bundled in bed, and both of his brothers happily at home, the only person unaccounted for was Claire.

And he couldn't shake the feeling that something was wrong.

"All right, what's bothering you?"

Evan glanced at Grant. "What do you mean, what's bothering me?"

"Well, something has you pacing."

"Maybe he's afraid of thunder," Chas said with a laugh.

"Or maybe he's worried about Claire," Grant suggested shrewdly.

"I'm not worried about Claire."

Chas spit out a laugh. "Lord, Evan, if I were you, I would be."

"So would I," Grant agreed without a second's hesitation. "Frankly, little brother, I'm at a loss to figure out why you haven't staked an official claim yet."

Irritated, Evan paced away. "Listen to you. You'd think this was the eighteen hundreds and Claire was some sort of land grab."

"All right, Evan," Grant said, exasperated. "You don't like tact, then I'll drop it. What's the deal with the two of you? Are you going to marry this girl, or do you plan on living in sin?"

Evan only stared at Grant. "*You* are the one who's nuts."

"Nope, I'm curious. And, frankly, I think I have a right to be. Hunter and I bid on that new shopping mall going up in the next county and we won. I'm here in Brewster for the next two years, while we build the mall and all the restaurants and ancillary shops. So what I'm trying to figure out is if I have a home, need a home, or should be looking for a home."

Before Evan could say anything, Chas sat up on the sofa. "Yeah, Evan, me, too. I decided the reason I've been so confused about my job offers is because I don't want to live in the city anymore. Not only is Arnie Garrett reaching retirement age, but Judge Flenner's not getting any younger, either. I'd be a fool to leave home when I have an opportunity right in my own backyard—that is, if I have a backyard. If you and Claire are going to get married and take the house…''

"What in the hell makes you two think Claire and I are going to get married?" Lord knew, he certainly hadn't done anything to give anyone that impression. And Claire had been quiet and pensive for the past several days, too. If anything, his brothers should actually think he and Claire disliked each other, not that they were planning a wedding.

"You can't hide the way you look at someone," Grant said, answering the question on Evan's face. "And you and Claire just have that kind of glow about you."

As if to prove them wrong, Evan glowered at his brothers. "Well, forget it," he said, a little more loudly, a little more angrily than he would have liked, then traipsed to the window again.

"She playing hard to get?" Chas teased.

"*She's* not playing anything."

"Oh, *you're* playing hard to get, then?" Grant observed, but there was a laugh in his voice.

"You guys are irritating idiots. Did it ever occur to you that I have enough on my plate right now without thinking about getting married?"

"Is this what you're telling Claire?"

"Actually, yes," Evan admitted, because he knew his brothers weren't going to drop this, and sometimes the truth was the best way out of an argument. Even if it was only half the truth. "I have a mill to run. Almost every person in this town depends on us for their livelihood. And if that isn't enough, I have triplets to raise."

"*We* have triplets to raise," Grant reminded quietly. He slid down in his chair and tented his fingers against his chin. "What you're telling us, then, is that you're not getting married because you're too busy?"

The wind picked up. It roared around the side of the house and rattled the glass panels behind him. Evan cast a furtive glance toward the window. His intuition screamed that he should worry, that something was wrong.

He licked his dry lips. "It's more than that. I'm not sure I love her. Don't you think that having the kids and the business wouldn't matter if I really loved her? So since they matter, I guess I don't love her."

"And that would explain why you're having a heart attack watching the storm," Grant suggested shrewdly.

"I'm not having a heart attack."

"Okay, a stroke, then," Chas said with a laugh.

"I am not having a stroke."

"Then what are you doing? We're perfectly safe. The only person not here is Claire. So, she's got to be the one you're worried about."

Tired, confused, Evan slumped on a chair.

"Evan, we both know you're lying to us," Chas said. "I suppose it's your prerogative if you want to bear the burden of a problem alone. But don't lie to us. Just tell us to butt out."

"All right, butt out."

"Okay, I'll butt out," Grant agreed, rising from the chair behind the desk. "However, before I do, I want to make sure you understand that you can't use the mill or the babies as an excuse. Now that both Chas and I have agreed to stay in town, you don't have any excuses. You and Claire could go anywhere you want. Do anything you want."

But he couldn't. Evan knew he couldn't. And he

was tired of people interfering, pretending to understand problems and emotions that no one could understand unless they'd lived them.

"Are you done?" he asked quietly.

Grant nodded. "I've had my say."

"Me, too," Chas agreed.

"Fine," Evan said, then strode out of the room. The wind shook the house again. Ignoring it, Evan jogged up the steps toward his room. But because he had to pass the nursery, he paused. In the end, temptation overcame him and he tiptoed in to make sure all three babies were undisturbed by the noise. Assured they were sleeping soundly, he leaned against Cody's crib and stared at him.

He knew why he didn't tell anyone he couldn't have children. It was because no one understood. If he had confessed to Grant or Chas, neither one would have taken it seriously. They would have laughed and joked about not having to worry about paternity suits. But even if they had taken it seriously, they would never know the depth of feeling awakened by discovering you were sterile. Worse, one or both of them might have offered the suggestion that he adopt or maybe that he marry a woman who wouldn't mind submitting to artificial insemination.

To a person who could have children, either of those alternatives solved his problem. The trouble was, when you were the person who couldn't have kids, the value of paternity came into much clearer focus. He didn't want kids for the sake of being a father. He wanted kids for posterity, continuity, for the chance to see himself in another human being. For the chance to give something to the world.

Every time he really thought about not being able

to have his own children, he felt inept, incompetent, worthless.

Pointless.

And anytime anyone suggested an alternative method, it only rubbed salt into the wound.

Chapter Eleven

Claire waited three days and gave Abby's suggestions serious consideration before she actually acted on them. Then she called Grant and asked if both she and Evan could take a night off from the triplets and he enthusiastically agreed.

With her plan securely in place, Claire slowly made her way into Evan's office at the end of the day on Tuesday. "I have a surprise," she said quietly.

He raised his eyebrows, but didn't say anything.

"I'd like you to have dinner with me—tonight—at my apartment."

This time, he only stared at her.

"We've never really been alone," she ventured, her voice trembling because she knew she couldn't handle the humiliation if he turned her down. "And I just thought it would be nice for a change to act like normal people."

When Evan stayed quiet for a long time, Claire felt a sinking sensation in the pit of her stomach. She had the horrible sense that she'd said something wrong, but Evan drew in a long breath and said, "You're right. We never did have a chance to act like normal people."

"Well, here's our chance to fix that. I made lasagna last night. All we have to do is heat it. We could have a quiet dinner, uninterrupted by diaper changes or dropped toys, and then we'll talk."

When he stayed silent again, Claire said, "Even if the offer of an evening with me isn't all that exciting, at least a night without having to pick up toys should be worth something."

At that Evan laughed. "I love those kids…"

"No one's saying that you don't. I'm only saying we could both use a night away."

"Grant and Chas do think I'm taking everything a little too seriously. It would serve them right if I didn't come home tonight."

It was on the tip of Claire's tongue to tell Evan that she'd already made arrangements with Grant, but she decided against it. Though it wasn't like her to withhold a truth, if defying Grant gave Evan motivation to come to her apartment, then she wasn't going to argue.

When he arrived on her doorstep, she took the wine he had brought, and it hit her full force that this was Evan. She'd invited him to her apartment and he'd accepted. Now he stood at her door, still dressed in his dark suit, white shirt and tie from work, handing her wine…like a real date. And she didn't even have her shoes on because she'd absently removed them when she arrived home.

Nervous, she rubbed one stocking-covered foot over the other and clutched the bottle. "Thanks."

He smiled. "You're welcome."

Little butterflies took flight in her stomach. All afternoon she'd fretted about how she'd bring up the fact that she'd solved their problem. But with him standing in her apartment, close enough to brush against, comfortable enough that he might just touch her...or kiss her...or take her in his arms and make love to her...she swallowed. Suddenly, nothing seemed easy.

Evan wasn't a hundred percent sure why he'd accepted her invitation except something about her had changed. She was different, quieter, more mellow or something. Though he knew he was teetering on the brink of another broken heart, he harbored the ridiculous hope that she wanted to tell him she'd come to terms with his problem, she'd accepted it, and she wanted him anyway.

So here he was. Hoping against hope she could accept him, and itching to touch her, to kiss her...anything. Knowing the possibility existed that she could love him as he was, knowing that this time tomorrow she might be his, he felt impatience nudging him. But he controlled it. This was her show.

"I'll get glasses," she said softly, and turned to go into the small, orderly kitchen.

Evan followed her.

As she set the bottle on the center island, she said, "Dinner's just about ready."

He heard the tremor in her voice, knew she was nervous and stifled a laugh. They were probably on the brink of the most important conversation of their lives, and though he understood that she'd be fidgety, he felt nothing but excitement.

She grabbed two glasses and a corkscrew from the

cupboard and brought them to the island, where she struggled to open the bottle. Evan didn't interfere, but eventually she gave up, glanced at him and smiled.

"I seem to be all thumbs this evening," she said timidly. "Would you mind doing this?"

"No problem," Evan said, taking the bottle from her hands.

She nervously flitted away, grabbed a mitt and opened the oven door to reveal her dinner. Wonderful, spicy scents drifted over to him, but Evan was preoccupied with the fact that Claire was taking long, deep breaths. He suspected she'd turned away thinking he wouldn't be able to see. But she was breathing so hard and so deeply that he wondered if she wouldn't soon hyperventilate.

He set the wine on the island, took the four steps that separated them in two long strides, grabbed her by the shoulders, spun her around and planted his mouth directly on hers.

When he released her, she only stared at him for several seconds, then she slapped him with her oven mitt. "You scared the life out of me. Why the hell did you do that?"

He smiled. "You're not nervous anymore, are you?"

"No," she said, but she gripped his shoulders as if she'd slither to the floor if she let go.

Knowing it was patently untrue, Evan with tongue in cheek said, "I was just trying to make you comfortable."

Believing him, she took a long, calming breath, then pressed her head to his shoulder. "Thanks."

The rightness of it sneaked through Evan's devilishness, warming him, giving him that euphoric feeling again. He'd never known anything that felt so good, so perfect. He almost couldn't believe it when a low voice of doubt whispered in his ear that he shouldn't be taking anything for granted. It annoyed him so much that he decided he wasn't merely going to ignore it, he was going to override it.

He kissed her again. Why? Because he needed to be sure he hadn't imagined everything he felt the first time. Confirming that he hadn't, hope, confidence and power enveloped him. He pulled away, turned her around and patted her behind.

"Now, get me dinner," he commanded, knowing that eventually she'd catch on that he was teasing her.

"You're ridiculous," she sputtered, and pulled the piping-hot lasagna from the oven. "I hope you don't think I'm impressed by the Tarzan routine."

"Nah," he said, leaning negligently against her counter, watching her, enjoying her, telling himself to remember every detail of this night. "But I do think you're impressed by a really good kisser."

"Oh, now you're pushing it."

"Would you like another demonstration?"

She dropped her spatula. "No."

"Scared?"

"Hungry," she replied haughtily. Lasagna in hand, she stuck her nose in the air and marched into her dining room.

When she turned around, he was right behind her. "So what you're actually saying is that you acknowledge the fact that if I really got to kissing you, we probably wouldn't get back to the food."

She gaped at him. "What is with you tonight?"

He wanted to tell her that he was in love. That he was teasing her because it felt so damned good to be normal. Instead, he only grinned at her. "That's really funny. I was just about to ask you the same thing."

"I can't imagine why," Claire said, brushing past him to go into the kitchen to collect dishes and utensils. "I'm not the one who's acting silly."

"You don't think so?" Evan asked, again right behind her when she turned from her silverware drawer. Though he'd deliberately trapped her between his body and the cupboard behind her, he acted as if there wasn't anything amiss. "To me you've been behaving just this side of peculiar all day."

He watched a nervous tremor ripple through her and couldn't tell if it was a response to the idea that she might have made a fool of herself, or if she was reacting to him sexually. Lord knew, he was reacting to her. He loved the game, he loved the chase, he loved playing with her. He loved *her*. He loved the way she blushed. He loved the way she sputtered when she was flustered.

Seeing that her hands were full, he bent down and kissed her on the mouth again. He heard a piece of silver clatter to the floor, withdrew and walked into the dining room.

She cursed.

Evan smiled to himself.

He decided not to do anything else noteworthy until he'd given her a chance to have her say. He recognized that his impatience might ruin everything so he pulled back, ate his food, complimented her cooking, drank the wine and tried to listen while she talked about everything under the sun except her and him and sex.

Not that he was preoccupied with sex. Though he appreciated the fact that she was the first woman he'd really *wanted* since he discovered he couldn't have children, their relationship was founded on much more than the physical. Unfortunately, right at this minute, the physical end of things was demanding a little attention.

He pulled his foot out of his loafer and almost touched the tip of his toe to her stocking-covered foot, but as if her arch had eyes, she bounced from her seat. "Would you like some coffee? I have chocolate cake for dessert and there's nothing like coffee with chocolate cake."

"I don't really think I want dessert."

Claire smiled at him. "Really? That's odd, you look like you're still hungry."

With another bright smile, she pivoted and walked into her kitchen and Evan drew in a long, frustrated breath. If he looked like a man who was hungry, there was a damned good reason for it.

She returned carrying two slices of cake and two cups of coffee on a tray. "We can eat these here…or on the sofa," she said innocently, but Evan could swear he'd heard a hint of something in her voice.

Telling himself not to argue with success, he rose from his seat. "The sofa would be nice."

She nodded. "More comfortable," she agreed solemnly, leading him into her living room. She set the tray of coffee and cake on the table in front of the sofa and offered him a seat.

He sat, thinking that this was definitely, absolutely, positively the luckiest night of his life, but just as quickly as some R-rated visions began dancing across the screen of his mind, other important facts interrupted like special bulletins. Number one, she was a virgin. And number two, he still wasn't sure what her intention was for inviting him here tonight.

Best to get number two out of the way before they discussed number one.

"So, Claire," he said, taking the plate she handed to him. "I know you thought I needed a break and that's why you invited me here, and I appreciate that," he said, sounding like the normal, intelligent, rational man he was. "But I suspect there's something else on your mind."

"There is," she agreed casually, reaching across him to get cream for her coffee.

When she stretched, he could have sworn she deliberately brushed the skin of her arm against his hand, causing him to have to suppress a surprised jerk, but he couldn't prove it. He certainly couldn't have made a clear decision from her demeanor. She looked as innocent as a kitten, sipping her coffee.

He narrowed his eyes.

"But I just want to be sure you're comfortable first." She pulled a pillow from behind his back, plumped it and angled it behind his head. Unfortunately, when she did that, she also slid her fingers along the fringe of the hair at his nape. She blew in his ear. Neither motion was clear enough to prove, but they were deliberate enough to elicit a very explicit reaction from him.

"I'm fine," he growled.

"And are we done playing games?"

This time, when his eyes narrowed, he looked at her. "You are bad."

"*I'm* bad?" she gasped, but then she giggled. "I thought I was going to swoon at your feet twice."

"It's nice to know I haven't lost my touch."

"It's nice to know I'm finding mine," Claire countered, every bit as confident as he was.

Evan smiled. "It's also very nice to see I haven't overestimated you."

Claire pinched his cheek. "Honey, you haven't seen anything yet."

He returned the favor. "I'm counting on that...after a little bit of a discussion."

She sighed. "Okay, you're right. We need a discussion because there are certain things you need to know."

Confused, Evan stared at her. "Why did you say that as if what you're about to tell me is a bad thing?"

"Because I'm not a hundred percent certain you're going to think it's a good thing."

"You're not sure I'm going to think your acceptance is a good thing?"

"No. I'm sure about that part..." She gave him a sly look, reminding him that he'd more than shown her his feelings by kissing her three times before dinner. "It's the other part that concerns me."

The little voice of doubt returned. He told it to take a seat, but it insisted on sitting in the forefront of his brain. He swallowed. "You want to marry me, right?"

"Absolutely," she said, laying her fingers against his cheek.

He turned his face into the warmth of her hand and pressed a kiss against her palm. "You love me, right? You're not marrying me out of pity."

That made her laugh. "That would be the day."

Because he agreed, he laughed, too. The little voice of doubt protested, reminding him that if he continued to avoid the issue it wouldn't do anyone any good.

Knowing he had to obey the voice of doubt eventually, he sighed heavily and asked, "So what's the problem?"

"It's not really a problem," Claire said, using a tone that Evan knew was relieved, positive, optimistic.

He felt a moment of relief himself, but the voice of doubt brought him back to reality.

"It's a solution."

"A solution? Claire, I can't have kids. I've had all the tests. There are no solutions."

"Of course there are, silly," she said, and snuggled against him because he'd laid his arm across the back of the sofa. "For one, we could adopt."

He stiffened.

"For another..." She sounded slightly afraid again, and Evan understood why, because he knew what she was about to suggest. "There are all kinds of ways you and I could get a child."

Fury overtook him by degrees. Not because her suggestions were so terrible, but because of what they represented. "Don't you think that I'm smart enough to recognize there are hundreds of ways I can get a child? I don't want to get married only to have children. What I want is a woman who can love me."

With that, he bounced from the sofa and strode to the door. "I thought you loved *me*," he said, then stormed out into the night.

Chapter Twelve

Seeing how angry he was, Claire wasn't about to let him leave. Not only was he bubbling with emotion that would make driving hazardous, but she was certain that he had somehow misinterpreted what she'd said. She'd offered them a solution. Yet, he'd acted as if she'd insulted him. She couldn't let him go until they straightened this out.

"Evan, wait," she called, running down her porch steps to his sport utility vehicle. "Wait."

Though she could tell he considered ignoring her, he didn't. In fact, as she picked her way across her gravel driveway in her stocking feet, she could also see he got himself under control.

"I'm sorry," he said as she stopped in front of him.

"No, I'm sorry," she countered, refusing to let him take the blame, which was just a way of avoiding the real issue. She hadn't forgotten that he never really wanted to talk about this. Tonight she would find out why if she had to spend all night cross-examining him. "I could see my suggestion upset you. Abby said—"

"Abby? You told Abby?"

"No. No," Claire said, shaking her head. "I gave her a hypothetical situation."

"Oh, like she's not going to guess it's me," he said. Exasperated, he combed his fingers through his hair. "Can't you see I don't want this problem advertised all over town? I don't want anyone to know. It's a miracle that I told you. I wouldn't have, except you needed to know because not being able to have children is part of who I am. If I hadn't told you, you might have fallen in love but it wouldn't have been with me. And that's the real issue. You can't accept me. I don't want you to have to sacrifice and do all kinds of crazy things to work around my deficiencies. I want you to love me. Exactly as I am. Deficiencies and all. If you can't accept me—without children— then you don't love me."

Claire took a pace back. "I can't believe what I'm hearing. I think the truth is, you don't love me. You're so focused on you and what you want, you don't see me at all." She stared at him, then whispered, "It almost seems that you're not looking for someone to love, you're just looking for someone to love you."

"I think it's one in the same thing."

"It isn't. Not really," she said, her heart splintering with pain. "I don't know how I could have been so stupid," she said, then turned and ran up the steps to her apartment.

Evan followed her. He grabbed for her arm twice, but Claire quickly jerked it out of his reach. She opened her apartment door and closed it before he had a chance to get in behind her.

* * *

"What's this?"

When the white envelope was slapped down on the desk in front of him, Evan peered over his shoulder at his older brother. "It looks like a letter."

"By God, it is," Grant said, his voice low and sarcastic.

Evan narrowed his eyes. "All right. What's going on?"

"Why don't you tell me," Grant said, yanking his father's high-backed chair from the desk and almost depositing his brother on the floor. If Evan hadn't been so quick on his feet, he knew he would have been sitting on the carpet right now.

Instead, he bounced out of the way when Grant took the chair he'd been occupying and eyed him imperially.

"Claire isn't coming over to help with the kids tonight."

Though that troubled him, Evan didn't show any emotion. "She wasn't at work today, either."

"Guess what? I know that because that letter is from her."

Glancing at the letter, Evan swallowed.

"She's resigned."

Still keeping his reactions to a minimum, Evan took a slow, quiet breath. "I had a feeling she might."

"Oh, how nice. You had a feeling she might."

"Grant, this isn't any of your business."

"The hell it isn't," Grant spat, leaping out of his chair and grabbing Evan's shirt collar in his fist. "I like Claire...and so do you."

If Grant hadn't been holding his shirt collar, Evan would have bolted. "Stay out of it, Grant."

Grant only continued to study Evan's eyes.
"Claire's too loyal to tell me what really happened.
You're too damned stubborn. But I'll bet Abby
knows."

Evan swallowed.

Grant released Evan's collar. "I think I might just
pay me a visit to the diner."

"Don't!"

"Abby knows, doesn't she?" Grant surmised
shrewdly.

Evan drew a long, deep breath. "Yes."

"Then I think you'd better tell me unless you want
me going into town, stirring things up."

"Grant, please, this is my life."

"What about your life?"

Evan didn't answer, but when Grant reached for the
doorknob he knew he had to. He tried to gather some
courage. It didn't come. "Grant," he said simply. "I
can't have kids."

"What?" Grant gasped.

"I can't have children. That's why I can't marry
Claire."

Grant slowly lowered himself to one of the wing
chairs by the sofa. "How does Claire feel?"

"It's very complicated. She's too young to make
this kind of choice..."

"Did you tell her that?" Grant asked incredulously.

Evan took a long, deep breath, feeling this hadn't
been half as difficult as he had imagined it would be.
"Yes."

"And she didn't slap you silly?"

"Claire's not naive."

"No, but she loves you," Grant said, then shook
his head. "Evan, I'm having trouble reconciling some

of this. I'm trying to understand your feelings, and though I don't think it's completely possible, I do think I have a handle on your side of things. But Claire doesn't strike me as the kind of woman who'd refuse adoption…or other means for having children.''

Just when he thought he had finally found someone who understood, Evan was once again hit with the reality that no one would ever understand. He bristled and pulled back his emotions before he did something foolish like admit his pain and humiliation. ''I never asked Claire to do either of those things for me. I would never ask anyone to sacrifice like that for me.''

''You've completely lost me,'' Grant said.

His temper snapping, Evan faced his brother. ''Then let me spell it out for you. Every time I've dated anyone over the past few years, I couldn't get my mind off how they'd react when they discovered I couldn't have children. I'm not just cursed with being sterile. I've lost the joy of my youth, my innocence, my future. Now, you can tell me it's selfish. You can tell me I'm wrong. But I want somebody who's going to love me for me, not explain how she's going to get children in spite of my deficiencies.''

''Claire loved you. Claire *loves* you.''

''No.''

''Because she wants children?'' Grant asked incredulously.

Evan felt a stirring of foolishness, but tamped it down because Grant was taking everything out of context. ''You're confusing the issue.''

''No, I'm not. You're telling me that because she wants children and has found an alternative, you took that to mean she didn't love you.''

Evan swallowed. "That's not how it was."

"Then explain it to me," Grant said, congenially opening his arms. "I'm all ears."

"You don't understand."

"Of course I do," Grant said calmly. "Your pride is wounded, so you're punishing someone else."

"I am not punishing her."

"Well, you're certainly not acting like a man who loves her."

"Maybe I don't."

"Good," Grant said, suddenly sounding supportive. "Because I've asked her to work for me and Hunter."

"What?"

"Claire is dedicated and hardworking. I asked her to help me and Hunter set up the field office for the new mall project."

Evan didn't say anything, only stared.

Grant lounged in his chair. "Yeah, it'll be great. She's agreed to be here by seven every morning, and to continue to help with the kids.... Oh, but since the two of you have problems, she'll be watching the kids with me and you'll be teaming with Chas."

Evan felt a swift stab in his heart, and with every sentence Grant said, the knife twisted. Because he realized Grant might be setting him up, he refused to react. In fact, two could play this game. "That's great. I don't like the idea of Claire being without work. I appreciate your taking care of her."

"Good, it's a deal, then," Grant said, rising from his seat and ushering Evan out of the den. He more or less pushed him into the corridor, then closed the door.

Standing in the middle of the downstairs hall, Evan looked around. He'd won that. He knew he had.

So why the hell did he feel so confused, frustrated…angry?

Angry. Deep down, soul-burning angry.

Chapter Thirteen

Evan watched Claire arrive the following morning.
Dressed in jean shorts, a snug T-shirt and little white
tennis shoes, she looked like a woman ready to do
manual labor. He frowned, annoyed that his brother
might be so thoughtless. He didn't believe Grant
would actually force her to do heavy labor, but he
had said he'd hired her to help set up a field office....

Slapping his hand on the windowsill, Evan
scowled. He knew what Grant was doing. He also
recognized Claire might be in on it. They wanted him
to admit he loved her, so they were going to throw
all kinds of stupid scenarios in his way that would
tempt him to admit his feelings.

Well, guess what? His feelings were strong and
deep. Claire's feelings were the ones in question. All
he had to do was remind himself of that every time
he wanted to interfere. All he had to do was remind
himself that the first time he really opened himself
up to a woman, offered himself to a woman, she

basically refused him. She'd focused on the children issue and compromised.

"Good morning, Claire," he said cheerfully, when she opened the door and walked into the foyer. Jogging down the last three steps of the circular stairway, he added, "I'm glad to see our little problem didn't affect your decision to take the job with Grant."

"So am I," Claire said quietly. "Particularly since he doubled my salary."

Evan's eyes widened. "He what?"

"He doubled what you were paying me," Claire said matter-of-factly. "If I didn't know you as well as I do, I might have thought you talked him into that. But since I know exactly how you feel about me, I know this offer from Grant is genuine." She looked him right in the eye. "And I'm taking advantage of it."

He might have been happier if she'd been a little more hurt and a little less angry. Just as Grant had done, Claire had obviously put the blame on him.

Well, fine.

"I'm glad you did," Evan said, smiling to let her know he could and would handle all this.

"That makes two of us," she announced, then started down the hall to the den.

Confused, irritated, Evan stared after her, but only a few seconds into watching the sway of her hips, the swing of her shiny dark hair, the long length of leg exposed by her shorts, he realized he wasn't angry anymore. He also realized he was thinking pleasant thoughts about her.

He stamped them out and turned to go into the kitchen. Unfortunately, Annie began to cry. Thinking

Grant would get her, he again took a step toward the kitchen, but she didn't stop crying.

"Grant?" he called.

No answer.

"Chas?"

No answer.

No big deal, he thought, and pivoted toward the steps. He would simply grab her himself. On the way down the hall, he heard the sound of the shower and realized that Chas was probably getting ready for the day. When he walked into the nursery and found all three babies still in their cribs, he decided Grant was preoccupied with setting up his field office and had forgotten about the kids.

One by one, he took the babies from their cribs. He bathed them, strapped each in a seat and gave each a toy. When all three were ready for breakfast, he checked to make sure they were safe, then headed for Chas's room.

"Hey, I need some help with the kids."

"Sorry, buddy," Chas said apologetically as he rummaged for socks. "I've got an interview with Judge Flenner this morning."

"No problem," Evan said, and backed out of the room. "I'll get help from Grant."

Before going downstairs, Evan checked on the kids, saw they were okay, and ran down the steps. "I need help," he said as he stepped into the den. To his surprise, Claire and Grant were bent low over the mahogany desk. When he stepped into the study, they broke apart like guilty teenagers.

Feeling the heat of anger surge through him, Evan cleared his throat. "I need help," he said evenly.

"Sorry, Ev," Grant apologized slowly, and Evan

couldn't tell if he'd apologized for not being able to help or because Evan had caught him trying to steal his girl. "But we're swamped this morning."

Not wanting to show a reaction to the fact that Grant was moving in without so much as a decent mourning period for the relationship he might have had with Claire, Evan forced a smile. "No problem. I've handled the kids alone before," he said, then slipped out of the room.

He managed to get through the breakfast without a hitch, even phoning his new secretary to let her know he'd be late. Without reminding anyone he would have to call off for the entire day if someone didn't soon help him, he settled himself in to care for the kids, because as far as he was concerned, this was his main duty. This was also what he'd been trying to explain to Grant and Chas a few nights ago, but they refused to listen. Neither Grant nor Chas had the sense of responsibility he had, and these babies needed him. Of course, the mill needed him, too. But all things considered, the triplets needed him more.

By ten o'clock, with all three kids down for a nap and facing the prospect of feeding lunch to three screaming babies, Evan knew he was going to have to gather reinforcements. He called Claire's sister and her friend and asked them to watch the children for the rest of the day. Proud of himself, he was just about to walk down the hall and surprise Claire and Grant with the news that the girls had arrived and he was leaving for work, when Claire and Grant burst out of the den, laughing like teenagers.

Grant skidded to a stop. "Oh, hi, Evan."

"Grant," Evan said stiffly, not even bothering to hide his annoyance.

"We're going to the diner for lunch. Want to join us?"

He looked from Grant's happy face, to Claire's bright, shiny blue eyes and a heavy ball of emotion filled his gut. Not only was Grant perfectly happy to steal his woman, but the woman who was supposed to love him seemed to be more than willing to be stolen.

"I would join you for lunch," Evan said rigidly, "except I only now found someone to care for the kids. So I have to go in to work."

"Tough break," Grant said, and put his hand on the small of Claire's back. "We'll see you tonight."

With that he was gone. So was Claire. Evan picked up his briefcase and started walking to the door. He could hear Claire and Grant laughing on their way to Grant's truck, and the kids giggling with the two teenagers who were their afternoon caretakers. Suddenly Evan felt very, very alone in the world.

"More potatoes, Claire?"

As Grant catered to Claire's every whim and wish at dinner that night, Evan stabbed his steak with his fork, then began cutting as if he were sawing a log instead of tender beef. Rain beat against the wall of windows in the back of the dining room. Wind rattled the glass. They were in the midst of another storm, except this time Evan welcomed the noise, the wind and the chill of the rain. They mirrored his mood perfectly.

"How was work today, Evan?" Chas asked innocently, and Evan speared him with a look.

"It was fine."

"I was surprised to hear you'd hired someone to replace Claire weeks ago..." Chas began, but Claire interrupted him.

"He didn't hire Janine to replace me, exactly," Claire explained. "But we were lucky she was already there when I quit."

"I never did hear that whole story," Chas said to Evan, but Grant quickly answered.

"The mill is established, but my company's still growing. We all decided Claire would be more of an asset to me than to Evan. Right, Evan?" Grant asked, peering at Evan as though Evan were supposed to be pleased that he'd come up with a reasonable explanation—particularly since everyone knew he wasn't feeling exactly reasonable right now.

"That's right," he answered as cheerfully as he could. He knew what Grant was doing, but Evan was nonetheless putty in his manipulative hands. Because right now, he felt like hell and a heel. Guilt swamped him because he knew Grant was covering for him because he'd pushed Claire to quit. It had only now sunk in, but he finally understood that it would hurt Claire too much to work for him. Because Claire wasn't as good an actress as Grant was an actor, Evan could see the depth of her pain in her eyes.

He just couldn't do anything about it.

Didn't anyone realize that?

"I'm tired," he announced suddenly, and rose from his seat. "I'm going to bed."

"Okay, Ev," Grant happily agreed.

"Good night, Evan," Chas said.

Claire caught his gaze. "Good night, Evan," she said softly, and Evan felt the effect of every word.

She loved him. She'd never done anything but love him.

He fought the guilt. He fought the urge to even *consider* he might be the one in the wrong, and strode out of the room.

"Well, that didn't work."

"Tell me about it," Grant said, snatching a slim cigar from a box he kept in his father's desk drawer. He lit it with a quick flick from a lighter, then tossed the lighter to the desk blotter with a thud. "I don't think I've ever met anyone as thick-skulled and stubborn as your brother."

"He's your brother, too," Chas reminded, then fell to the wing chair by the burgundy sofa. "So, what do we do now?"

"Frankly, I'm out of ideas."

"But he's miserable," Chas argued. "Maybe we're using the wrong angle. Maybe we should be trying to get Claire to bring him around..."

Chas stopped when Claire entered the room. She'd been standing outside the door long enough to realize that they'd been working some sort of plan to get her and Evan back together again and it had failed. Though part of her appreciated that they cared enough about their brother to interfere, the other part was furious. She was so mad she knew her eyes were probably shooting sparks of fire.

"Chas, I don't care how miserable your brother is and I don't care how pathetic I seem to the two of you, I want you both to stay out of it."

"You aren't pathetic, Claire," Grant said, obviously trying to smooth things over.

"Oh, really? I suppose you double the salary of everyone you hire."

"What I'm paying you is the going rate in Georgia," Grant said, then crossed his heart. "Scout's honor."

"Baloney. I think you wanted to make sure I'd take the job so I'd be here today and Evan wouldn't have a chance to…"

"Oh, for pete's sake, Claire," Chas groaned. "Don't you dare even say Evan needs time to heal. What he needs is a good swift kick in the pants."

"Do you hear what you're saying?" Claire asked quietly. "I've never felt more like chattel than I have over the past few days. This problem involves more than Evan. Did it ever occur to either one of you that maybe I don't want him back?"

"No," Chas mumbled.

"No," Grant seconded, slumping in his chair.

"Did either one of you think to ask me how I felt about this whole deal?"

"No."

"No."

"Then stay the hell out of it," Claire said, and marched out of the den and out of the house. Not slowing her pace, she quickly made it to her car, strapped herself in and drove to the main highway. When she was about a mile away from the Brewster house, she pulled off the road and let herself cry. She'd never been so embarrassed in her whole life. But in spite of her own misery, she knew she hadn't been trying to save face back at the house, but trying to keep Evan's brothers from tormenting him for the next few weeks. The most humiliating part, though, was realizing she'd been tempted to take their help.

She'd been tempted because being that close to Evan and hardly speaking to him, let alone having an actual relationship, had been torture. And she couldn't handle it. She was ready to take him any way she could get him.

Fortunately, she remembered that she'd saved herself for twenty-three years for the *right* man.

If Evan Brewster wasn't the right man, no matter how much it hurt to lose him, then she had to let him go.

The storm picked up around midnight. Rain pummeled Claire's bedroom windows and lightning trimmed everything in gold. Even if she hadn't been miserable and upset, Claire knew she would have gotten no sleep. After a full hour of tossing and turning, she crawled out of bed, made a cup of cocoa, grabbed an afghan and curled up on her recliner. Two minutes before she would have fallen into an uncomfortable, exhausted slumber, there was a knock at her door.

Half-asleep, overtired, she actually answered without thinking. When she saw Evan standing on her porch, his hair rain-soaked, his collar turned up against the wind, his hands stuffed in the pockets of his jeans, she thought she was dreaming.

"Can I come in?" he asked quietly.

"I guess so," Claire said, and stepped out of the way so he could enter.

"There are about six or eight questions that I have to ask you, but before I ask anything, I have to know if what you told my brothers tonight is true."

"I told your brothers a lot of things tonight. Which one do you need clarified?" she asked groggily.

"Have we really made you feel like chattel?"

"Oh my God, yes," Claire groaned, finally beginning to fully awaken. "Ever since I've met you guys, I've been somebody who's helped and somebody you've needed, so I understood my place in your life was odd. But to have your brothers working behind the scenes to try to get me to change your mind was the straw that broke the camel's back. You'd think I wasn't a person with feelings, but just a convenience. It was embarrassing and demeaning."

"I'm really sorry about that."

"You should be. You *all* should be."

"Grant thinks I'm stubborn."

Claire sniffed. "Big news flash."

"He thinks I don't deserve you."

This time Claire caught his gaze. "Maybe you don't. I thought the same thing tonight myself."

"So, would it be pointless if I apologized and asked for another chance?"

"Actually, yes," Claire said, and busied herself with collecting her cocoa cup and saucer. She needed something to do with her hands. He looked wonderful and perfect, and all she really wanted to do was hold him. She wanted to feel all those wonderful sexual things he made her feel. She wanted to be his woman. But on her terms, not his. And since Evan Brewster was accustomed to getting his own way, she didn't think her terms would ever come into consideration.

She risked a glance over at him, saw the spark of hope in his beautiful green eyes and almost lost the battle. Reminding herself she had to be strong, she took her things to the kitchen.

"Have you investigated the other ways of having kids?"

"You make it sound ridiculously cold," Claire said, furiously rinsing her cup under the faucet. "And besides, this isn't about kids. It's about us. Damn it. I'm so sick and tired of everything in this relationship boiling down to that one issue that I could scream."

"So scream."

She whirled away from the sink and pointed a finger at him. "I should scream. I've known you for some time and in those months since I've known you I've had to convince you I wasn't in cahoots with Arnie Garret, I had to convince you to let me help you with the kids, and I had to prove I was competent at work. You, Evan Brewster, are a cynic."

"Pretty much."

"And I'm not going to marry a cynic."

Stifling a smile, he caught her gaze. "I never asked you to marry me."

"Good, because I won't. I won't marry you."

"Not even if I buy you a really big diamond?"

Something about his tone clued her in to the fact that he might not be teasing. About to issue a scathing retort, she stopped herself, her forehead furrowed, and she frowned. "I like diamonds."

"And here I thought you weren't materialistic."

"I'm not," she said, forfeiting her anger to confusion. "I just really like diamonds."

"I'll let you pick the one you want."

"At the expense of my sanity?" she asked sarcastically. "I don't think so."

"I'll keep my brothers out of your life."

"Oh, and make me seem like a shrew?"

Evan drew an exasperated breath. "Then what do you want?"

"I want you to act like a normal man who loves me."

"If I do that, we're going to be making love tonight."

Just the thought took her breath away. "Really?"

"Really," Evan agreed with a laugh, but he stopped suddenly and shook his head. "I never realized how difficult I was making things for you."

"Oh, things weren't so bad," Claire said, weakening. "Just every once in a while you got a little headstrong."

"And if we were married, and I did that, you'd settle me down?"

"You better believe it."

"Then I think we have everything settled."

Trying not to focus on making love, being loved, and living with this man for the rest of her life, Claire concentrated on her grievances to make sure he'd adequately addressed them. "Yeah, I think so," finally she said.

"Then we're going to get married."

She lifted her chin haughtily. "You just reminded me that you haven't asked."

"I'm asking."

"Asking what?" she said, because she wasn't taking this for granted.

"Will you marry me?"

She let the question settle in and warm her all over. She glanced at the clock to see the time. She listened for the comforting sound of the storm. She took a long, satisfying study of Evan's face, memorizing every detail, and then every detail of how bad he looked, how wet.

Recognizing he had to have been walking in the horrible, nasty weather for quite some time to be that wet, she sobered. "You're okay with this?"

Obviously realizing her seriousness, he said, "Yeah. Really, really okay with this."

"Then I'll marry you," she said, walking into his open arms.

* * * * *

Don't miss more exciting adventures with
THE BREWSTER BABY BOOM. *Look for
BRINGING UP BABIES, on sale in
February 2000, and OH, BABIES! on sale in
March 2000…only from Silhouette Romance.*

VIRGIN BRIDES

Join
Silhouette Romance
as the New Year brings new
virgin brides down the aisle!

On Sale December 1999
THE BRIDAL BARGAIN
by Stella Bagwell (SR #1414)

On Sale February 2000
WAITING FOR THE WEDDING
by Carla Cassidy (SR #1426)

On Sale April 2000
HIS WILD YOUNG BRIDE
by Donna Clayton (SR #1441)

Watch for more **Virgin Brides** stories from
your favorite authors later in 2000!

VIRGIN BRIDES
only from

Silhouette®
Where love comes alive™

Available at your favorite retail outlet.

Visit us at www.romance.net

SRVB00

If you enjoyed what you just read,
then we've got an offer you can't resist!

Take 2 bestselling love stories FREE!

Plus get a FREE surprise gift!

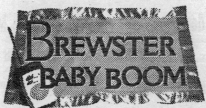

MONTANA MAVERICKS
Big Sky Brides

Legendary love comes to Whitehorn, Montana,
once more as beloved authors

Christine Rimmer, Jennifer Greene and Cheryl St.John

present three brand-new stories in this exciting anthology!

Meet the Brennan women:
SUZANNA, DIANA and ISABELLE

Strong-willed beauties who find unexpected
love in these irresistible marriage of
covnenience stories.

Don't miss
MONTANA MAVERICKS: BIG SKY BRIDES
On sale in February 2000,
only from Silhouette Books!

Available at your favorite retail outlet.

SILHOUETTE'S 20ᵀᴴ ANNIVERSARY CONTEST
OFFICIAL RULES
NO PURCHASE NECESSARY TO ENTER

1. To enter, follow directions published in the offer to which you are responding. Contest begins 1/1/00 and ends on 8/24/00 (the "Promotion Period"). Method of entry may vary. Mailed entries must be postmarked by 8/24/00, and received by 8/31/00.

2. During the Promotion Period, the Contest may be presented via the Internet. Entry via the Internet may be restricted to residents of certain geographic areas that are disclosed on the Web site. To enter via the Internet, if you are a resident of a geographic area in which Internet entry is permissible, follow the directions displayed on-line, including typing your essay of 100 words or fewer telling us "Where In The World Your Love Will Come Alive." On-line entries must be received by 11:59 p.m. Eastern Standard time on 8/24/00. Limit one e-mail entry per person, household and e-mail address per day, per presentation. If you are a resident of a geographic area in which entry via the Internet is permissible, you may, in lieu of submitting an entry on-line, enter by mail, by hand-printing your name, address, telephone number and contest number/name on an 8"x 11" plain piece of paper and telling us in 100 words or fewer "Where In The World Your Love Will Come Alive," and mailing via first-class mail to: Silhouette 20ᵗʰ Anniversary Contest, (in the U.S.) P.O. Box 9069, Buffalo, NY 14269-9069; (in Canada) P.O. Box 637, Fort Erie, Ontario, Canada L2A 5X3. Limit one 8"x 11" mailed entry per person, household and e-mail address per day. On-line and/or 8"x 11" mailed entries received from persons residing in geographic areas in which Internet entry is not permissible will be disqualified. No liability is assumed for lost, late, incomplete, inaccurate, nondelivered or misdirected mail, or misdirected e-mail, for technical, hardware or software failures of any kind, lost or unavailable network connection, or failed, incomplete, garbled or delayed computer transmission or any human error which may occur in the receipt or processing of the entries in the contest.

3. Essays will be judged by a panel of members of the Silhouette editorial and marketing staff based on the following criteria:

    Sincerity (believability, credibility)—50%
    Originality (freshness, creativity)—30%
    Aptness (appropriateness to contest ideas)—20%

    Purchase or acceptance of a product offer does not improve your chances of winning. In the event of a tie, duplicate prizes will be awarded.

4. All entries become the property of Harlequin Enterprises Ltd., and will not be returned. Winner will be determined no later than 10/31/00 and will be notified by mail. Grand Prize winner will be required to sign and return Affidavit of Eligibility within 15 days of receipt of notification. Noncompliance within the time period may result in disqualification and an alternative winner may be selected. All municipal, provincial, federal, state and local laws and regulations apply. Contest open only to residents of the U.S. and Canada who are 18 years of age or older, and is void wherever prohibited by law. Internet entry is restricted solely to residents of those geographical areas in which Internet entry is permissible. Employees of Torstar Corp., their affiliates, agents and members of their immediate families are not eligible. Taxes on the prizes are the sole responsibility of winners. Entry and acceptance of any prize offered constitutes permission to use winner's name, photograph or other likeness for the purposes of advertising, trade and promotion on behalf of Torstar Corp. without further compensation to the winner, unless prohibited by law. Torstar Corp and D.L. Blair, Inc., their parents, affiliates and subsidiaries, are not responsible for errors in printing or electronic presentation of contest or entries. In the event of printing or other errors which may result in unintended prize values or duplication of prizes, all affected contest materials or entries shall be null and void. If for any reason the Internet portion of the contest is not capable of running as planned, including infection by computer virus, bugs, tampering, unauthorized intervention, fraud, technical failures, or any other causes beyond the control of Torstar Corp. which corrupt or affect the administration, secrecy, fairness, integrity or proper conduct of the contest, Torstar Corp. reserves the right, at its sole discretion, to disqualify any individual who tampers with the entry process and to cancel, terminate, modify or suspend the contest or the Internet portion thereof. In the event of a dispute regarding an on-line entry, the entry will be deemed submitted by the authorized holder of the e-mail account submitted at the time of entry. Authorized account holder is defined as the natural person who is assigned to an e-mail address by an Internet access provider, on-line service provider or other organization that is responsible for arranging e-mail address for the domain associated with the submitted e-mail address.

5. Prizes: Grand Prize—a $10,000 vacation to anywhere in the world. Travelers (at least one must be 18 years of age or older) or parent or guardian if one traveler is a minor, must sign and return a Release of Liability prior to departure. Travel must be completed by December 31, 2001, and is subject to space and accommodations availability. Two hundred (200) Second Prizes—a two-book limited edition autographed collector set from one of the Silhouette Anniversary authors: Nora Roberts, Diana Palmer, Linda Howard or Annette Broadrick (value $10.00 each set). All prizes are valued in U.S. dollars.

6. For a list of winners (available after 10/31/00), send a self-addressed, stamped envelope to: Harlequin Silhouette 20ᵗʰ Anniversary Winners, P.O. Box 4200, Blair, NE 68009-4200.

Contest sponsored by Torstar Corp., P.O. Box 9042, Buffalo, NY 14269-9042.

PS20RULES

ENTER FOR
A CHANCE TO WIN*

Silhouette's 20ᵗʰ Anniversary Contest

Tell Us Where in the World
You Would Like *Your* Love To Come Alive...
And We'll Send the Lucky Winner There!

Silhouette wants to take you wherever
your happy ending can come true.

Here's how to enter: Tell us, in 100 words or less,
where you want to go to make your love come alive!

In addition to the grand prize, there will be 200
runner-up prizes, collector's-edition book sets
autographed by one of the Silhouette anniversary
authors: **Nora Roberts, Diana Palmer,
Linda Howard** or **Annette Broadrick**.

DON'T MISS YOUR CHANCE TO WIN!
ENTER NOW! No Purchase Necessary

Silhouette®
Where love comes alive™

Name:

Address:

City: State/Province:

Zip/Postal Code:

Mail to Harlequin Books: **In the U.S.**: P.O. Box 9069, Buffalo, NY
14269-9069; **In Canada**: P.O. Box 637, Fort Erie, Ontario, L4A 5X3

*No purchase necessary—for contest details send a self-addressed stamped envelope to:
Silhouette's 20ᵗʰ Anniversary Contest, P.O. Box 9069, Buffalo, NY, 14269-9069 (include
contest name on self-addressed envelope). Residents of Washington and Vermont may
omit postage. Open to Cdn. (excluding Quebec) and U.S. residents who are 18 or over.
Void where prohibited. Contest ends August 31, 2000.

PS20CON_R